Meeks

DATE DUE

JAN 0 2 2014	

Meeks

a novel by

Julia Holmes

Small Beer Press
Easthampton, MA

Small Beer Press
150 Pleasant Street #306
Easthampton, MA 01027
www.smallbeerpress.com
info@smallbeerpress.com

Distributed to the trade by Consortium.

Library of Congress Cataloging-in-Publication Data

Holmes, Julia, 1970-
 Meeks : a novel / by Julia Holmes.
    p. cm.
 ISBN 978-1-931520-65-2 (pbk. : alk. paper)
 1. Veterans--Fiction. 2. Totalitarianism--Fiction. 3. Political fiction. I. Title.
 PS3608.O4943544M44 2010
 813'.6--dc22
                            2010010092

Printed on Recycled Paper by Edwards Brothers.
Text set in Minion 12.

Cover art © 2003 Robyn O'Neil, detail from *Everything that stands will be at odds with its neighbor, and
everything that falls will perish without grace.* Blanton Museum of Art, The University of Texas at Austin,
Collection of Jeanne and Michael Klein and the Blanton Museum of Art, fractional and pledged
gift, 2004 (T2004.2.1/3-3/3). Originally Commissioned by Artpace San Antonio. Photo:
Richard Sanders, Des Moines.

To Lucy and Richard Holmes,
for the world

The Brother's Tale, Part 1
(September Prologue)

Early on the morning of Independence Day, I lay awake on the pile of old coats—castoffs from the Brothers of Mercy—and watched over my brother. We were still living in the small windowless room by the train station, a room to which electricity was so feebly supplied that we actually conducted our lives within an even smaller circle of light in the center of the room and used the grimy corners for kicking our boots angrily into something when we returned home from a day of work as civil servants. I worried that my brother and I were becoming just like the two brothers in the famous story about the two brothers marooned on an island together.

My brother was sprawled naked under the kitchen table; his face was swollen and dark with dried blood. The pliers lay nearby. The portrait of Captain Meeks gazed down disapprovingly from his place above the door. Empty bottles stood around my brother's head like concerned townspeople who had found their king unconscious in the street.

I could hear the boots of the Brothers of Mercy coming down the hall, kicking at the doors of civil servants throughout the building. *Thanks be to God! It's Independence Day!* I twisted the sleeve of my gray smock around my head in an effort to make them disappear, to unwind time and go back go back, and then I heard them drop the coil of rope outside our door. My brother's eyes slid open. He spewed vomit across the dusty floorboards and then closed his eyes again. The flies that had been studying his face jumped up and hung in the air, presumably full of hope.

I cleaned my brother's face with a damp cloth. Where the rotten tooth had been, the jaw radiated heat. "It's all this drinking," I whispered soothingly, in a tone that I hoped reminded him of our mother. I helped him into his gray smock and settled him in the kitchen chair, so I could work the air-dried, crusted socks of the workingman over his ice-cold feet.

I divvied up the last of the tea between our cups, filled the empty tea envelope with gunpowder, and then filed it away in the tea box. I turned back to the gas stove to light it. I listened to the *tick, tick, tick* of the sparker clicking, and I studied the wooden tea box, now packed with gunpowder.

"Today is the day, Brother," I said and smiled conspiratorially at him. He was hunched over the table, dribbling blood. Yes, a brother is a wonderful thing! But one eventually wants more out of life. I poured scalding water from the little pot we shared over the scant tea leaves and let them steep. How is it that the human being outgrows new pleasures so quickly, yet he can settle with such conviction into the most intolerable arrangements? I watched the steam rising from our cups; I heard a train, bound for the Sheds, picking up speed along the rickety tracks. The radio buzzed vaguely in one of the black corners of our room. Consider the unlucky housefly born to die in this room, never to know more of life.

My brother struggled to his feet and searched the dark corners of the room cursingly for his boots. I wrapped the tea box carefully in a canvas sack and pushed it to the bottom of our workbag. I put the fuse I had made from the laundry cord in my pocket and gave the box of matches to my brother, as a precaution.

We made our way to the execution. The streets were filling up with other civil servants, all of us pouring out of our gray holes into the austere blue light of the city in early autumn.

Out of the catacombs, here we come, an army of the dead resurrected to pour the punch!

Every few blocks, my brother spat a wad of blood-soaked cloth from his mouth and replaced it with another. Whenever the heavy coil of rope began to hurt his shoulder, he shifted it to the other. I carried our workbag, the tea box knocking ominously, awkwardly against my leg.

We hit the outer ring of heavy industry. The factories were operating at full power on Independence Day, and a thick white smoke chugged out of the old stacks and spread into a thin fog over the city. The factory courtyards were strewn with pink and yellow flowers blown from the embattled trees and ground into the asphalt by marching feet: the bedraggling of the living world come autumn. In the distance, I could see the high wall of the prison and beyond that the black-green line of the river.

The closer we marched to the heart of the city, the more beautiful the world was: the smell of the ash-dusted loaves of bread cooling in the bakeries; the crisp, clean autumn air and the harmless bell tones of the shop doors opening and closing block after block; the halved blood oranges arrayed on wooden spikes by the fruit vendors; the cherry-red taillights of industrious trucks idling in the street, the roadside weeds capped with sweet little flowers—even the garbage-eating birds were puffed up with health and self-love. Our luckier brothers and sisters swarming around us now, bright-faced and in a rush, chugging out plumes of phantom breath as they hurried toward the park. Boys and girls were chasing after the cake carts as they rumbled down the street, the police horses shaking their harnessed heads, jostling the silver-threaded tassels braided into their forelocks for Independence Day. Whenever a young woman passed, a surge of atmosphere . . . perfume or powder . . . and my brother would turn his head to watch her go, a deposed king sniffing the air, dragging his chains. I carried our workbag; my brother hauled our rope. Young women watched us indifferently: Two Civil Servants Doing Their Work. I shifted our workbag on my shoulder and felt the reassuring knock of the gunpowder box.

My brother and I climbed into the Great Tree and out onto the Reynolds Branch. As someone with a lifelong interest in the theater (I'm an artist, myself), I had already spent long hours thinking about Reynolds, the man who had carved his name into the living wood. Why had he done it? (Motivation) Had they hung him for his act of vandalism, or had he been the hangman? (Backstory) I touched the raised scar of Reynolds's name for luck as I crawled over it. Poor Reynolds, whoever he was . . . in our world, his name meant death.

My brother stowed the coil of rope, and I wedged our workbag carefully between two smaller branches. I could smell burned sugar and woodsy smoke, as if secret, smoky fires had been lit in the damp woods: the last of the icing pots being doused. I watched the families, those inviolate clusters of serene and healthy human beings who practice their craft in the spacious workshop of the family home and whose members boast expertise in all extremes—jealousy, resentment, devotion, concern—while my brother and I were two amateurs obliged to keep these emotions running on our own in a windowless room by the train station. I gathered all my worries to the lathe so that I could turn and turn and turn on myself. Was brotherly love enough—was it a sufficient source, or could a man such as myself, even burning the oil of it frugally and with utmost care, exhaust it? Would I end up alone? God, what had happened to us?

We were ordinary boys! Raised to be ordinary boys. We saved coins in the old coin box under the stairs so we could visit the cake carts in the park every Sunday; we pretended to hunt down the Enemy in the yard; we pledged our soft hearts to the Captain. Only this spring, my brother and I were among our brothers, in our pale suits. How had brotherhood collapsed to a mere pair of brothers? I scanned the crowd for bachelors so that I could stoke the hatred in my heart.

"Look at them," I said, spitting the words.

My brother shrugged.

I pretended to watch the Founders Play from my branch. I fixed an insipid, play-enjoying smile on my face and held the workbag casually in my lap. I worked the fuse slowly into the clamp I had fastened to the outside edge of the tea box. Though the air was cool, my undershirt was soaked in sweat.

The Chief of Police appeared onstage, and the people fell silent. The actor playing Captain Meeks started up the steps to the stage. I could hear the *thunk, thunk* of his boots on the hollow stairs. I touched my brother's arm, and he turned to look at me—oddly—as if we were becoming reacquainted after a long estrangement, and I showed him the fuse snaking out of the workbag and under my gray workman's smock.

"What are you doing?" he said, holding his jaw in agony as he spoke.

"I'm doing this," I said matter-of-factly, but I felt suddenly adrift. There's a kind of narrative discontinuity (at least in one's family) that can make a person feel that he is suddenly on the perilous outer edge of his sanity. What *was* I doing? I was doing this for my brother, for myself, in memory of my mother and my father. *Check*. I was doing it to make the guilty pay. I looked with disgust down on the people staring slack-jawed at the stage. *Check*. Then I glanced over the great gleaming length of the Independence Day cake, as wide as the park path and snaking for hundreds of yards through the park. I imagined the feel of the soft, white flesh of the cake against my tongue, the surge of sugar against my brain. I revolted myself: the hour of death was building my appetite. I laid my hand over the canvas sack, felt the edge of the tea box. All of us would simply have to be destroyed.

"Give me the matches," I said to my brother. He ignored me. "Matches, matches," I repeated in an intense, persuasive whisper, but he ignored me. I reached toward his pocket, where I could see the outline of the matchbox, and he slapped my hand away, and I reached again, and he hit me much harder, and I nearly fell from the branch. A few people had started to watch us and were laughing at our antics, laughing at us as if we were clowns—I mean, professional clowns.

"Fine," I said, "Let's just sit here and watch an innocent man get Reynolds'd." I hardly recognized my brother. He had the eyes of a viper and the soft, bloated face of a sick child, and I tried to remember that he was once a good-looking man with a sweet and forgiving nature. "Well, I won't let it happen," I said, but I wasn't sure what I was really capable of without him. Maybe my brother and I were just two ancient and retarded animals, new to New Creation but anciently equipped, warped only to each other. The actor playing Captain Meeks was deep into the standard patter now, and I was impatient for them to pull some poor condemned man to the stage so that everything else could happen.

I heard the condemned man gasp for breath as a policeman pulled the black bag over his head, plunging him into darkness. The Chief of Police glanced up at us, and my brother began lowering the rope. I held the coiled fuse in my hand as if it were a dead mouse that I had rescued and cared for and grown to love, and I whispered, "Matches, please, Brother, matches." He ignored me. I tried to think of all the things two industrious brothers could make from this enormous tree. I tried to calculate how many boards could be milled from the trunk, tried to remember how many floorboards were in the front room of our mother's house (I used to lie there for hours and count them).

It occurred to me that, momentarily, I would cease to exist in the mind of the condemned man. I was willing to blow my brother and myself into oblivion, but the thought of my extinction in this stranger's brain flooded my body with fear. "Matches, matches, matches, Brother." I was near tears. My brother ignored me. I begged the truth to come into my mind, and I promised to do whatever the universe required of me if only it would show me the way. The Chief of Police lowered the noose over the condemned man's head. My heart—that once-powerful organ!—pounded indecisively beneath my gray smock, and the evening bells filled the air, solemn and beautiful to all of us, and I saw that the condemned man tilted his head to listen.

Young Man! This ship is sailing:
Happiness bound. Cool tide, mild light,
The soft green ground seized and taken—
Let others see that you know where you are going.
To the orchard, let us go, where your
Brothers and Sisters are waiting.
There we neither save nor hoard, for all that we need
Is forthcoming.

Ben

The alien silhouettes of a New Family drifted behind the gauze-thin curtains of his childhood home. He knew by heart the route that blocks of sunlight took when they migrated along the upstairs hall; he knew the sound of water traveling through the walls to meet his mother's face when she washed for bed; he knew the smell of his father's suits in the armoire. As a boy, he had loved to hide in the armoire between his father's suits, inhale the scent of the cedar planks slotted into the pockets. In the evenings, he had rolled a coin silently across the high kitchen counter while his mother made him dinner, and he had reached out to touch one of the ice-cold plums bobbing in a bowl of water. "Leave them alone," his mother had said, and he had returned to rolling the coin, slowly, moodily, along the high wood counter.

There should be signs of a struggle: uprooted trees,

trenched soil, shattered windows, charred stone, bleeding policemen crying pitifully in the yard, the odorless corpses of Brothers of Mercy piled high in the drive. That was the mother he remembered: the merciless protector of all that was hers and his. But he had left her, and maybe she had simply grown old in her fortress of tea and warm wool, easily conquered by the Brothers of Mercy, by a polite, insistent knock at the door. Another day, another old woman who clutched at her frail heart and screamed, "Mercy!" when bulbs blew overhead or pots overboiled, who feared everything from her morning shower to the common household peril of stairs to the slow, dragging knock of a stranger at the door: *The countryside will do you good, Sister.*

Ben stared hard at the old house, and the old house smiled serenely back at him without recognition. The windows glowed benevolently around the shapes of the invaders. The flower beds were thick with life. A house was a beast of burden all too happy for new masters.

Ben yanked a flower from the low-hanging branch of a flowering tree in the yard and walked on, past the garbage sorters whose hands moved like independent animals, past the gray-faced laundrymen harvesting the crisp white shirts of other men from the line. Ben pinched the stem of the flower reassuringly between his thumb and finger: the fruit carts, the stalwart police horses, the warm and glowing windows of the factories by the river—*his* city, everything as he had left it.

Down the street, the old butcher was still in his shop, hard at work, hunched over a low scale before the same gleaming walls of yellow tile, the same affirming cherry-red and mint-green lights that spelled out CITY BUTCH-R. Ben loved how the dusty neon lights tinted the butcher's folded white paper hat, loved the crispness of the butcher's white apron, blood-pink fingerprints notwithstanding. He sighed with pleasure, felt his body relax. The sky was clear and bright, and it was still early in the summer, and maybe it was true that almost anything in this world could be regained, and almost anything could be made.

Across the street, Ben went into the slope-floored old shop and found the tailor standing at his enormous work-table eating fried fish with his fingers. Ben thought of his mother, frightening and sweet, their summer by the sea.

"Ben!" said the tailor with the cheerful indifference of an old man. Behind him, dress dummies bristled with pins; fabric hung from every available bar, hook, and nail; regulation suit patterns, tattered and constellated with pin pricks, slumbered neatly beneath the tailor's worktable. The tailor wiped his fingers on a scrap of fabric.

"I was very sorry to hear about your mother."

Ben nodded. "Thank you."

The tailor circled, inspecting the condition of Ben's military uniform. He approached once or twice to eye the stitching, yanked gamely at the cuffs. "Look at this handsome soldier. Looks like the uniform held up well."

"Well, for the most part . . ."

"That's all behind you now, Ben. You must look to the future!" Against the far wall of the shop, pale cardboard boxes stood in stacked columns; the tailor pulled a box expertly from the middle stack: "Try this."

"Is there a changing room?"

"I'm not your mother, Son. Just put it on. And give me back your uniform."

Ben turned his back to the tailor and changed quickly. He could smell the cheap black dye of the suit when he opened the box; he saw the pant legs were creased horizontally at the knees, where they had been folded, for years, probably. It was depressing, the cheap black suit, the columns and columns of cardboard boxes filled with cheap black suits, but he supposed it was designed to be depressing: the apparatus of grief. Ben tucked his military cap back into his satchel and turned to face the tailor.

"You see, Ben? Problem solved. It's the clothes that turn boys into soldiers, soldiers into men."

Ben sat in the worn armchair at the front of the shop and sipped tea the tailor had made for him. He watched the butcher at work across the street. The heavy, dusky shapes of meat hung from the ceiling chains, their shadows stock-still along the yellow wall. The butcher hauled a rack of ribs from the glass case; he forced the thin blade between the ribs and sliced them apart.

"They've reassigned the house," Ben said suddenly. "Another family is living in it. I saw them."

The tailor turned, concerned, "Did they see you?"

"I don't think so," said Ben. "Then I came here."

"You should have come here first, and I might have prepared you for the shock." Ben touched the warm side of the porcelain teacup and shrugged apologetically. "And now you've nowhere to go." The tailor sighed, hesitated. "I know of a Bachelor House—an excellent one. Nine-tenths marry out in the first year. Something like that. I might be able to get you a room, but it won't be easy, Ben."

"I'd be grateful."

"Anything for your mother. I like to think I was a great comfort to her while you were away. She was all alone in that big house. And she was a great comfort to me, of course. Both of us waiting for our sons to come home, something you know nothing about."

Ben opened his mouth to speak.

"This is no time for formalities, Ben. Let's not explore our feelings, shall we? Time is of the essence for a man like yourself, but here you are, still youngish and, in any case, an eminently marriageable man, and I wouldn't worry too much. Nor would I put *anything* off.

"Listen to me carefully." The tailor brought over a small wooden chair and sat uncomfortably close to Ben. "Are you listening?"

"I'm listening."

"For the moment, you should make the most of grieving—you'll only have one opportunity in life to grieve for your own mother. Don't cheat yourself. Remember, there is no instinct for comporting oneself around death; grief won't come to you whole and perfectly formed without some work on your part. Your instinct may be to go insane, to hit yourself in the face, to tear out your hair, to cry all the time, to scream at the sky, to run into the river, to blame others, even to attack them in the full fever of grief." (Ben opened his mouth to speak, but the tailor raised his hand to stop him.) "If the dead man or woman is a close relative, mourning is expected—in all other cases it isn't. If required to mourn"—he pointed at Ben, Ben nodded—"get a black suit, preferably one as dark as night. Done. In speech and attitude, be as inconspicuous as possible. What is grief but a sudden inability to sustain belief in the story that preceded it? I say you're lucky. Only those who have grieved love the world enough. I try to picture the missing sleeping peacefully, like those smooth rocks in the shallows of a clear, cool river, the water soothes them, it soothes them. . . ." The tailor brushed the air in a gentle arc and smiled peacefully. "I like to imagine some birds singing to the water. This may be a comforting thing for you to think about." The tailor leaned back in his chair and frowned at the view of the butcher's shop through the window. "Did you know that long ago—too long ago for any of us to remember—this entire street was lined with tailor shops? Anyone could stumble in off the street and ask for anything, no matter how ridiculous. No guidance, no rules, no comprehension of the stakes. You're lucky to be living in this day and age, Ben, when good, hard-working people can expect to succeed, when happiness comes to those who deserve it. Do you appreciate how lucky you are?"

"I do," said Ben.

"Good." The butcher stepped out into the street and lit a cigarette, blinking in the strong sun. Ben and the tailor watched him from the window. "You're a good boy, Ben. It's honorable, at least, to engage one's father's enemies. Look at you—taking up arms against the Enemy, when so many of your brothers will raise a fist only to defend their own happiness."

Ben smiled noncommittally.

"The butcher's son—there's a perfect example of what I'm talking about. He stole another man's suit last summer, right off his living body. The police caught him, of course, swung him for the crowds." Ben glanced across the street; the butcher shuffled back into his empty shop, started halving and quartering the racks of ribs.

The tailor leaned toward Ben. "What have you got in terms of cash?"

Ben reached into his satchel and handed the tailor a folded stack of bills. "Only this," he said. The tailor weighed the money unhappily in his hand before pocketing it.

"How quickly can you make a new bachelor's suit?" asked Ben.

"I can't make you a new suit. It's out of the question."

"But everything in the house is gone, including my father's suits. I have nowhere else to start but here."

"You *have* a suit. I just *gave* you a suit, Ben. The ingratitude of bachelors in this day and age never ceases to amaze me."

Ben glanced down at his new black jacket, more of a bottomless gray in the light of the window. "And I'm grateful for it—thank you. But I'll need to buy a pale suit, in addition."

"Impossible. I'll have to put all the money you gave me toward paying your bills at the Bachelor House."

"I'll get more money."

"How do you plan to do that? You've got nothing to sell, and you can't work until you're married."

"Couldn't I owe you the money? I'll pay you back once I'm married, have a job."

"No."

"For my mother," pleaded Ben, hating himself.

"But it's for you, isn't it? Not for her, so let's not confuse matters. If I made a suit for every bachelor who begged me, Ben, I'd soon be out of business and living in a little room by the train station and cursing my 'fate,'" said the tailor, raising his fat fingers to indicate quotation marks around the word. "Give up my life, so you can have what you want? As I said, it's out of the question."

Ben stood and stretched. He should think strategically. Always better not to push old men. The tailor returned to his worktable; Ben investigated the tailor's dummy in the front window of the shop. The dummy was wearing a classic bachelor's suit, the sleeves pinned behind its back. A hat had been laid over the neck, giving the dummy the look of a commanding officer deep in thought, his chin against his chest, his hands clasped peacefully behind his back, as he paced some ridge over a smoky, blue-gray field of battle. "Beautiful suit," Ben said. "They can't make them like this any longer, can they?"

"But we most certainly can still make them like that, and do." The tailor stared into the pool of fabric, pressed a scrap of fabric against the back of his neck to soak up his sweat. "It's already getting hot as hell."

"I have an idea," said Ben. "Could I use this suit? Rather than asking for a new one." He smoothed his hand across the fine pale fabric.

"No. It belongs to someone else."

Ben saw that years of shop dust had accumulated on the brim of the hat. "But if he isn't coming back for it?"

"But he is coming back, Ben. He is coming back, and he will need his suit."

The tailor turned his back to Ben, began petulantly re-arranging the scraps of cloth on the table.

"I'm sorry," said Ben. He stared dumbly at the back of the old man but was paralyzed by uncertainty. He might easily make things worse while intending to make them better. The tailor's son had been missing in action for as long as Ben could remember—twenty-five years, at least. Finally, the tailor turned and pointed at him. "The black suit is more important, Ben, for those observing you are unlikely to read the subtler signs of grief. Is it artificial? Of course it is. But how else will you communicate your feelings, Ben, when conversation in this city is so dishonest and exhausting."

Meeks

I made my rounds first thing in the morning so that I wouldn't miss Bedge, who sometimes came to the bench early. I had a serious matter to take up with him, something that couldn't be postponed. I hurried around the perimeter of the park, checking the fence, shaking the park gates to test hinges and locks, and then cut back down through the center, taking note of the condition of the statues and monuments, giving special attention to the statue of Captain Meeks—the father of our world (and my namesake). I was in a hurry, but once or twice I found myself standing, still as a statue, in a clearing or under a tree, mesmerized by the blue bud of summer: the river mist warming like wool under the first sun, the ants and beetles commuting along their branches, the worms boring silently through the new green leaves. The garbagemen were already up and trawling the park, and I felt their dead eyes slide over me as I stood stock-still in the sun.

Move along! I said. As you can see, Brothers, I am alive and well.

I went to the bench and waited. In the distance, the factories hummed with power, chugging white smoke. I heard the low, long morning whistle, and the great windows filled with light, and I tried, in vain for the millionth time, to make sense of the procession of shadows suddenly sweeping across them. Machines? People?

The fruit vendor set up his cart nearby, collapsing the delivery boxes and arranging the fresh fruit, pyramiding the limes . . . the plums, plump and purple-black, flecked with lavender, and the oranges constellated with fine drops of cool water, and the lemons bright and indomitable in the sunlight, and the polished red apples still bristling with dark, sweet leaves. A breeze rushed through the high branches of the park trees. I thought of how pleasant it would be to line the interior of my head with layers of the cool green leaves. I thought of how I loved the healthy green give of the grassy slopes, the sound of the breeze through the grass growing uniformly on the surface of the earth, the warmth emanating from it, the perfect scent of things just broken open. I love this world as I loved my very mother.

The fruit vendor brought me a few warm, soft plums wrapped loosely in some old paper. The day before, the baker had thrown a sugar bun my way. I took it from my coat pocket and halved it carefully, arraying the pieces neatly beside the plums.

That morning, as of yet, nothing had changed for me, so I was content watching the people coming in and out of the park, the people for whom things were under way. Their ships had sailed, and they smiled in the ship's breeze of an amiable open sea, and they smiled at the sights and sounds beyond the ship's rail, and they were people who were *launched* and it was a pleasure to watch them inhabit their pleasures without embarrassment. Young bachelors were leaning on their elbows along the green, sunny slopes, the young shadows of the trees overlapping in the grass, mild yellow nectars burning on their wicks, young women strolling in and out of lemon-yellow bands of sunlight, while the bachelors lounged in the shade like kings. Newly hatched, innocent and soft and warm, from the hulls of their houses, their heads swimming with dreams about the future: the face of a young man hangs like a pocket watch in his father's fog-choked silver shaving mirror, the face of a young woman hangs like an apple in the yellow haze of her mother's hand mirror. Mystery of mysteries: people alone in their houses. Perhaps it seems wrong for a mere policeman to feel such proprietary love for the society he watches over, but this was my world, as much as anyone's, and a policeman can be forgiven for thinking of his beat as his kingdom and the citizens as his subjects.

Meeks!

I jumped, discombobulating the plums. I arranged them again on the old paper, and Bedge sat beside me on the bench, looking out over the park and the clusters of new bachelors, comparing their suits and whistling after women.

Another summer, another season, Bedge said and sighed with a sort of contented resignation.

Plum? I asked.

Bedge poked one of the ruptured plums I had laid out for him. No, thank you.

Bread? I said, offering him half of the sugar bun.

Um, no. You have it, Meeks.

Are you sure you won't have something? I said and scooped up the old paper so that the plums and bread were floating conveniently right in front of his face. I had counted on my offering to lay the foundation for congenial negotiations.

No, no. Nothing for me, he said. But I've brought something for you. He removed his policeman's cap and said, I'm getting a new hat today—I thought you might like this one.

I need a gun, I said, moving directly, if awkwardly, to what was foremost in my mind.

Absolutely not.

But I am a policeman.

Meeks.

Bedge.

Why do you need a gun?

Why does anyone?

Which is precisely why we don't issue guns left and right, among the people.

I meant: why does any policeman?

Shall I take the hat away, if you don't want it?

No, no, no. I do want it.

Allow me, said Bedge, laying the hat upon my head as if it were a crown and then yanking it down, almost to my ears, with inhuman force. Now you're the very picture of a policeman.

I smiled uncertainly; my hands, having developed a kind of panicked free agency, flew to the sides of my head and tried uselessly to loosen the cap. The *hat*, I gasped, trying to give a name to my discomfort and confusion. Bedge ignored me.

You and I have a lot in common, Meeks. Considering our differences. Our situations couldn't be farther apart— me the Chief of Police, you the . . . (he seemed to search for the word) . . . rookie. But we share a requirement to be students of life.

Yes, I said, struggling as politely as I could against the efforts of the new hat to separate me from my body.

Bedge said, Do you remember the man in the black jacket?

I forgot the hat immediately. Man in the black jacket? I said. Man in the black jacket!

Bedge didn't answer me at first. He crossed his arms and stared petulantly into the distance. Perhaps he had thought that I would react to this news by nodding sagely and gratefully in my new hat, reflecting philosophically on the name of the ruiner of my life.

Apparently he's back in the city, said Bedge, trying to punish me, I suppose, by skipping over several lines of delectable back and forth that might have transpired between us.

Back in the city? I realized I was right up against Bedge, and I had compressed the plums and bread between us. He looked down at his juice-stained trousers with disgust.

Relax, said Bedge and pushed back me back down the bench to my regular spot. I won't tell you another word, he warned, unless you get a hold of yourself.

He took everything from me, Bedge.

I know the story well, Meeks. And now I'm telling you that the man in the black jacket was spotted in the city this morning by one of my men. Listen to me: If you see him, you must come find me. Do you understand?

Stay here. Find him. Get you.

That's right, said Bedge and patted me on the shoulder as he stood to go.

I looked down at the flattened plums, the stained paper, the golden quarry of the uneaten sugar bun—and I wanted none of it. My mind was busy spooling out the razor wire of an old hatred, coiling it mercilessly around every thought that entered my head, until my head was full of bad blood, and the whole day had gone.

The civil servants were collecting and folding the green-slat park chairs and sewing them together with thick, padlocked chains, and the people were drifting home to peaceful family dinners, to low lights, to quilts and cool, clean sheets and soft pillows, to glasses of refreshing night water. I stayed in the park, of course, having nowhere else to go. I waited for the evening bells to sound. I saw the lights go on in the street cafés. I smelled smoke from the cigarettes of the waiters, who smoked outside in loose ties before the dinner hour.

I made my way to the statue of Captain Meeks. I unlaced my boots and coiled the laces into my coat pockets. I unwrapped my feet and hung the foot cloth over a low branch. I struggled pointlessly with my hat, which seemed to be glued to my head, and then stretched out on my back under the fluttering black leaves . . . the boundless heaven at night. I felt better lying there beneath the Captain, just as my mother always did and once had, when I once wasn't was. *I once wasn't was.* The phrase swam drowsily through my brain. I could hear the garbagemen, always the last out of the park, making their way toward the gate, stabbing at garbage with their garbage stabbers. The smell of their cheap apple tobacco faded, and then it was just Mother and me again, me on the surface of the earth, her slightly under it, gazing past the tops of the nighttime trees just as we always had, when she would take my hand and speak directly into the vastness of space and say, My son will be the greatest of sons.

Ben

In the face of immediate disappointments, a person must take stock of the advantages that remain. He had a room at a reputable Bachelor's House; that was promising. He was lucky to be home in early summer; he was lucky to have the friendship of the tailor. One way or another, he would soon have a fine pale suit: he would devour the ground with long strides, yank apples from leafy branches and bestow them upon women in the park; he would kick the dew from the weeds that lined the streets, and women would drop their cups of tea, their smooth slices of iced lemon cake would topple from their plates and collapse on the grass, and his would be a vector of desirability cutting through the daily rounds of all women everywhere—transactions disastered, paths abandoned, children neglected, as the young women of the city were swept up in the fleet shadow of his apparently oblivious perambulations. But Ben would be long gone, walking on, preoccupied by work on an eternal problem.

Ben imagined two piles of men in the tailor's brain: the nameless, numberless bodies he had dressed, and, in the other pile, the tailor's son—and Ben. An advantage and a peril, to be so close to the tailor's heart.

Ben reached the Nines, the row of Bachelor Houses along the north side of the park. He stopped to watch a city muralist at work on the freshly plastered sidewall of a Bachelor House. A classic scene: the river a ribbon of blue sateen, the bright green of the park trees, the towering buildings laying gray and ghostly parcels of shadow along the smooth, clean grand avenue, and, curling over the horizon, the vast and open sea.

The artist ticked his brush lightly along the edges of the waves of the harbor to give them an optimistic trim of white foam uncharacteristic of the dark, sluggish swells one could see from the city. Through the clear blue waters of the mural sea, Ben could make out the shapes of ancient creatures.

"There's a whale!" he observed, delighted.

"Yes," said the painter gloomily. A whale stared up at them benevolently from behind the blue-green veil of water.

"My great-grandfather used to see them in the harbor," said Ben. "Hard to imagine."

Ben could see sailors on the ships that bobbed in the fresh white surf, the needlelike masts bristling, the shapes of people at ease in the park or bustling along the grand avenues, and along the edges of every scene, the murky figures, shadowantine, ashamed, the gray laborers armed with their pronged garbage stabbers, stabbing at scraps of shadow along the periphery. Ben recognized the scorched terrain of the opposite bank, and his heart sank: the Enemy's Territory laid to waste. He returned his gaze immediately to the beloved city. There was the statue of Captain Meeks peering from his great height through the trees; there were the bachelors, perfectly suited, at ease and as if facing an eternity of ease; there were the shapes of young women pouring into the park through the main gates. He looked again at the wrecked land across the river. A few preserved tufts of hard green forest where he had soldiered, the black masts of the Enemy's ships sunk in the rocky shallows.

"What's this—the black smoke on the ridge?"

"Soldiers' camp."

"And what about this smoke here?" Ben pointed to the inland wilderness beyond the train station.

"Listening Party. Bachelors around the fire."

"Much better," said Ben and reached out to touch the lovely curls of pale smoke.

"Please don't touch," said the artist and grabbed Ben's wrist.

"Sorry," said Ben but continued to reach.

Ben found the number on the street: Bachelor House 902. A solid white house, fissures in the plaster facade. Dark gray shutters. Rows of windows orderly as paintings on a wall. The window boxes were faded black, empty or soft and disorderly with wild grasses. Ben saw a face hovering in an upstairs window; he bounded up the front steps so the other bachelors could see his strength and his ambition, and be defeated, put down their smoldering cigarettes (he mustn't smoke, he mustn't smoke), stop harvesting silk ties from the tie-trees in their rooms, in order to worry.

Ben stepped into the dim entry hall; he could smell

cold grease and the loamy stench of long neglect. After a moment, he could see a loose boot tongue on the floor, one or two sun-bleached postcards, the edge of a coin wedged between the floorboards. Just pass through, he instructed himself—this is but a necessary passage, and life is waiting just beyond it. A man must suffer the confines of this life in order to reach the spacious enchantments of the next. Ben edged forward uncertainly. At the end of the hallway, he could make out the silhouette of an old-fashioned clock hanging over the fireplace, cool and shadowy in the warm spring air.

Another bachelor stepped into the hallway, smiling in shirtsleeves.

"Hey. I'm Albert."

"Ben," said Ben. Albert stepped up to shake his hand. Ben took note of Albert's thin, uneven beard.

"The tailor said we should expect you," said Albert, yanking self-consciously at his beard. "Let me show you your room."

"I like the beard," Ben said, tapping his own clean-shaven chin.

"Oh, thanks. You know . . . new development."

Ben glanced into the open rooms as they walked through the labyrinth of hallways. Young, intent bachelors—the tall, the hunched, the fat-faced, the over-groomed—alone in their rooms, honing their bachelor skills: one bachelor stood on a ladder with a paintbrush, painstakingly filling out the trompe l'oeil trees with fragments of green; another bachelor smoked a pipe and carved a bear's head out of a wet block of plaster (he glared up at Ben as he passed, the stem of his pipe clenched in his teeth); a bachelor pinned insects into a canvas-lined collector's box, pausing to brush the folded wings of his specimens with a soft brush, as if soothing them to sleep. As it was for Ben, it was for them: beneath the necessary intensity of mastering a bachelor skill churned the real restlessness, the great and thrilling imprecision of desire.

Ben wanted to be home, at home in a warm, unregulated place, with the background family fountain of talk, little talk, talk, little talk, and orderly tables suddenly disorderly with the passing of plates. Until then: pushups, statistics, scrimshaw—enviable craft! Albert looked back to smile reassuringly—he looked so young. Ben was not as young as he once was. What if he had waited too long? He had been forced by duty to postpone things and now had to work from the disadvantageous location of a Bachelor House where illness could spread quickly through overcrowded halls and where the defeatist routines of ailing and luckless bachelors in adjoining rooms could demoralize, and even an ambitious bachelor might soon find himself falling into a malaise. At which point, a doomed man (not himself, Ben soothed, but someone else) might die very quickly, even suddenly, perspiring alone in his room, or at the hands of the police, or as a thrown-away man, a worker in the various factories by the waterfront that milled foodstuffs and pumped fresh water and slaughtered animals and electrified the night streets and who knew what else, horrible and communal, until one died of exhaustion or was yanked from the factory floor by the trailing teeth of some awful machine, as had once happened to a friend's unmarried uncle. A loveless, childless man chewed beyond recognition and what did it matter?

A short, fat bachelor, seeing them pass, bounced up from his bed and swung out into the hall. "Hey there, Brothers! Can I give you a hand?"

"We're good, thanks," said Albert and took Ben's elbow,

pulling him along quickly. "Hurry," Albert whispered, "he's practicing."

"What's his thing?" asked Ben.

"To be the nicest guy ever," said Albert snidely, and opened a door off the hall. "Here we are."

Ben stepped into a small white room, the grooves of the molding softened and deformed by a thousand white-paint repaintings; through the square window he noted the desolate window box.

"Toilet's down the hall, one per floor."

Ben noticed another door in the room, the brass knob bent, the white paint around the knob smudged darkly with fingerprints. "Closet?"

"No, no, no. Sorry—better leave that alone. It's another bachelor's room. Not ideal, I know, but under the circumstances . . ."

"He has to pass through my room?"

"Technically, yes. But he never goes anywhere, so I wouldn't worry too much. Finton—one of the old-timers. I think he moved in last summer and has hung on."

"There isn't another room open?"

"Nope. But you'll get used to it."

Ben surveyed his new room, Albert's footfall retreated down the hardwood hall. The standard-issue bachelor's things: the battered armoire, the writing desk, the wooden chair, the narrow bed, the water pitcher. Not standard: the disconcerting door. Ben struggled to open the lone window, and then gave up, resigned to the stuffiness of the room, the heat of the days to come.

He fished in the satchel for his honeybee cufflinks and set them side by side on the little desk. Symmetry was not the least pleasure. He unpacked the bundle of canvases and unrolled them on the bed. His paintbrushes and tins of pigment, which had been rolled into the canvases, he set aside. The canvases were stiff with the still-life paintings of his prewar days. He studied the old efforts with dismay: the beloved objects of his mind's eye deformed by his idiot hand. He despised them.

At the center of each painting was his father's military cap, somehow salvaged from the shipwreck; the gold, honeybee cufflinks he had inherited from his mother's father; and a bowl of fruit—apples or mangoes or clementines or bananas—whatever he could bring to mind, the fruit being the variable he had permitted himself, the thing that required him to close his eyes and draw upon a reservoir of private thought. He heard a floorboard creak behind the strange door and froze . . . silence.

Ben flipped one of the old paintings over on the desk and sat down to face the blank canvas. He arranged the cufflinks carefully on the brim of his father's military cap. He took a pencil from the satchel. He tried to enter the orchard of his mind—Lemons? Apples? Plums? He should start with something that made him feel capable. Apples? He closed his eyes. The pencil rested in his hand, and soon he was wandering aimlessly through his thoughts. He imagined strolling along the rows of fruit trees in a beautifully tailored pale suit. He could see the shapes of women hurrying down parallel rows, women hidden by the thick green branches of vague trees. Ben tried to part the veil of leaves to see them better. Soon he was in pursuit, ignoring the slow-growing fruit along the boughs, until his body interrupted him with some complaint, and he noticed the tree leaves rustling outside and the ivy pressing against the sealed window of his room, and something important, circling his thoughts, remained remote. He dropped the pencil on the canvas, disgusted with his incapacity—he must not put off all that must be done.

Ben stretched out on the hard, narrow bed. It was only his first day in the house—he could easily launch himself in the morning without shame. He rested his head against the faint bleach smell of his sleeve and fell asleep in the heat. He dreamed he was lying on his back in the park, his black suit fading to pale gray in the sun, his eyes open and staring as the shadows of men and women walking past brushed over him like the blades of a fan.

When he woke it was dark, and the windowpanes shook slightly in their frames, as a light wind preceded a summer rain. He could hear the rain start against the windowpanes. The hall light shone under his door, and he could hear footsteps in the hall, doors opening and closing. He could hear men's voices—low, loud, pedantic, jocular, earnest, threatening. Bachelors. Sporting, gregarious, capable bachelors! Ben turned to the wall and pressed his hands over his ears, making an oath to reform in the morning.

Meeks

In the middle of the night, three men shook me awake. The park was cast in milky light, moonlight fused with the pale gold light from the old park lamps, the air was cool and clean. The men stood shoulder to shoulder. Behind them, clouds drifted like ghostly ships across a black and tranquil sea.

What do we have here?

A policeman, I said thickly, my brain larded with sleep. Officer Meeks!

The three men chuckled, then an awkward silence. They

stood over me. I saw that one of the men had only a thumb and ring finger on his right hand. It seemed to me that they were hesitating, unsure of how to proceed now that the universe had granted them something so far in excess of their dreams: a policeman.

They stood around me, one shuffled his feet, another spat at the ground.

Officer Meeks, repeated one of the men, to amuse the others.

Yes, I said, pretending to be bored. But some part of me was glad that they were there. There's the kind of loneliness that's a genuine fortress, and there's the kind of loneliness that wants anyone—one never knows which kind one has until it's too late. The man missing the fingers knelt beside me and smacked me across the face, and I heard a soft thump, my head striking the base of the Captain's statue.

The smallest of the men carried a metal bucket and a paintbrush with a long wooden handle and black bristles. Crab-hand and the third man (he wore a dark, rumpled suit and said nothing) pinned me against the grass, their knees digging into my shoulders. Crab-hand's disconcerting grip took hold of wrist. I couldn't see the faces of the men as they leaned over me, blocking the moonlight, becoming silhouettes bearing strong smells, chemical and bodily. I struggled for the sake of theater, until I thought we were all satisfied, and then I stared into the black river of the air, watched clouds drifting like majestic ships overhead. The milky light dissipated again, and the air turned cold. I could hear the faint sound of the brush scraping along the coarse material of my coat. I pretended that a lioness was licking my lapels, my chest, and the length of my body with her great rough tongue. (A mother is not shamed by any part of her son.) I could feel the pressure of the brush on the most vulnerable parts of my body. I could hear the laughter of the men, and then the asthmatic hacking of the man in the dark suit. He wheezed and spat, and Crab-hand tightened his awkward grip painfully on my wrist. I watched the sky fill up again with soft, white light, siphoning through the treetops. The strong smell of the paint, acrid and chemical, made me feel faint.

After a while, I sensed that Crab-hand was kicking me in the side, and the other two men were laughing, until the third man launched another round of coughing, and we all watched in silence until he backed away and pulled himself together.

Remember your place, said Crab-hand and spat at my face.

Remember my place? I said as coolly as I could. (Simple repetition is usually one's best defense.)

Crab-hand raised his horrible hand to hit me again, but then we all heard voices and laughter, mirthless and bristling with violence, the sound of our brothers, the Brothers of Mercy. The criminals ran. I, for one, seemed to be paralyzed. I could neither sit up nor see clearly, and then the voices dissipated and disappeared, and I was alone again.

I'm an officer of the law! I shouted at nothing, and the wind blew hushingly through the leaves. Don't shush me, I said. I'm not a boy.

I reached out in the darkness, and I laid my hand over the lush little hillock where my mother lay. Bedge and I had buried her there once, and there she had stayed.

The next morning, I crossed the park to the police station. I had done my best to scrape the lewd paint from my trousers and my jacket, but the ghostly outline of what they had done was only more suggestive for having been distorted, and it turned heads. To anyone who smirked or commented, I shot back, I'll remind you that I am a policeman.

I waited patiently for Bedge in the front room of the station. He emerged from a back room drying his hands on a small white cloth. His jacket was off, and his sleeves were rolled past his elbows.

Meeks.

Bedge, I need to speak to you privately.

We're all your brothers, Bedge replied, in keeping with tradition, but he walked over and stood close so that I would not have to shout in front of the others.

I need a gun, I said.

Bedge shook his head disapprovingly and told me to follow. He walked behind his desk. I stood at attention before him. Things were becoming more regular by the second.

I need a gun, I said again.

You're upset—have you forgotten?

Forgotten what?

Today's your birthday.

Is it? (What a pleasant surprise.)

You'd forgotten, said Bedge smiling fondly, and he opened his desk drawer and pulled out an apple, polishing it on his sleeve before handing it to me. I dug my teeth savagely into the apple, forgetting everything else. I was starving.

Bedge was silent for a moment before adding, I remember that your mother always gave you apples on your birthday.

Then I had to stop chewing and could only shake my head, the pulp of the half-chewed apple lodged in my throat. I craned my neck and stared into the rafters of the police station, trying desperately to master the wave of grief that was trying to swallow my brain.

Yes, I finally managed. She knew how much I loved apples.

A rookie who was filing papers in the cabinet behind Bedge's desk said, Son of the apple woman loves apples, but Bedge silenced him with a wave of his hand. This wasn't the first time I'd heard my mother identified as such, and as always, my mind was seized by a beautiful, mercantile vision of my mother, energetic and upright beside a portable stove in the park, her thick, dark hair filling with the steam of apples cooking in one of our two copper pots—everyone loves a steamed apple filled with butter and brown sugar, and I could see my mother consoling the inconsolable, young and old, in the steam of crisp, sweet apples each fall.

We're waiting for a new shipment of guns, said Bedge, pulling me from my daydream. Maybe next summer we can get you a gun.

Can I use yours until then?

Certainly not, said Bedge and tapped his holstered pistol lightly with his thumb. A nervous habit, very in the ordinary, but a gesture nonetheless that filled me with some trepidation. He said, Why don't you file a formal request now, and that way, we can issue you a gun as soon as they come in.

Good, I said, I formally request a firearm immediately. I watched his restless fingers drumming the side of his pistol. Bedge sighed heavily again, reached into his desk drawer, and withdrew a stack of forms. Interdepartmental Requisition Form 7898, he said. I forgot the nervous hand and holstered gun instantly.

But I'm a police officer, I said incredulously.

We spend our lives filling out forms, Meeks. Bedge settled into an old wooden office chair with metal wheels.

He rolled to a filing cabinet against the wall and kicked it with the toe of his boot. To a policeman, he said, anything not written never happened.

I tried to settle into this new arrangement of the facts, to remove all emotional signals from the surface of my face. Bedge, I said, I am an officer of the law, and I was attacked.

Why didn't you say so? Who attacked you?

A coughing man, a man with a crab's hand, a man in a dirty suit. A wave of cold-hearted rookie laughter passed through the station.

Have a seat, said Bedge, and pointed to one of the simple, wheelless wooden chairs scattered throughout the station. I pulled over a chair and sat across from him.

What happened, Meeks?

I need a gun.

Bedge pounded the desk with his fist. The rookies in the station froze like sweet-faced deer in a glen. Bedge folded the requisition forms, creasing them with angry precision, and shoved them into my pocket. Bring these back when they're done.

I don't have a pen, I said.

Of course you don't, said Bedge, and fished one out of his desk drawer. He sat emphatically back in his rolling chair and kicked off from the corner of his desk, crossing the front room of the station with an uneven series of clicks.

Ben

Ben stood naked in his unbearably hot little room and poured drinking water from the pitcher over his head. The bathroom down the hall had been overrun, men hunched two deep over a single aluminum sink, scrubbing their faces, soaping their greasy forelocks, grabbing for handfuls of ice-cold water. A broad-backed man shaved in a sheet of polished aluminum, dragging the blade along his chin. His reflection glared at Ben, who had retreated immediately to his room. Now he was using his pillowcase as a scrubcloth, and he washed himself furtively, nervously, watching Finton's door. He had dunked his underwear and his socks in the water pitcher when he woke in the middle of the night and had laid them out to dry. They had only grown warm and fetid in the humid little room, and he pulled on the damp underwear with disgust, and he put on the thin, black suit, and he forced his damp socks onto his feet and into his boots. He glanced out over the street now filling up with bachelors. Stirred by Ben's breath, a fly buzzed, zigzagged frantically against the glass, then fell black and plump into the corner of the window.

Ben headed downstairs, pushing self-consciously through the hall, already crowded with fit young men in pale suits. They were so much younger than he remembered bachelors being, so much taller, louder, better looking.

He was relieved when he saw Albert in the living room; he was studying his beard in the broken mirror over the mantel.

"Albert."

Albert jumped, adjusted his collar in the mirror, beads of sweat rolling from his hairline, through the patchy beard and into the cotton collar of his shirt, already damp with perspiration.

"Morning, Ben." Albert turned from the cracked glass. "Oh, my God—you're wearing that suit?"

"The other suit's not ready," said Ben, his face suddenly hot.

"Do you know when?"

"Soon," said Ben. "The tailor said it would be soon."

Albert pressed his handkerchief against his forehead and against the back of his neck. "Hope so. Let me know if I can help."

Ben thought immediately of *The Impostor*, the famous painting of a young bachelor lying dead on the stage, a violet thistle lodged in his throat.

Albert smoothed the lapels of his pale suit. "This was my father's suit," he said thoughtfully. "The tailor took it in for me. Dad was an enormous man. What about yours?"

"He died in the war when I was a boy."

"Sorry. I meant his suit."

"They reassigned the house while I was away. Everything's gone."

"Then the Brothers of Mercy probably gave your suit to some other bachelor. If I was walking around, and I saw some random guy wearing my father's suit, personally, I'd want to kill him."

Ben stared, unable to think.

Albert continued, "But the tailor's working on a new suit, so you'll be fine. You're different. There are other men here who've given up, good as dead."

"But it's just the beginning of the season."

"Right, they're not dead yet, but they're *as good as dead*—that's the distinction I'm trying to make," said Albert. "Obviously, they're still as alive as you and I, wandering the house, making sandwiches. But pretty soon, one or two will start to give off the stink of failure."

Ben stepped back, conscious of the smell of his dank underclothes, the faint chemical smell of his cheaply dyed suit. Albert went on in a conspiratorial whisper, "Yesterday in the park, I saw your roommate, Finton. He was a lying in the grass, barefoot, pants rolled to his knees, shouting at the sky. Poems, I think. Anyway, I gave him a piece of my mind—there's the reputation of the house to consider. And do you know what he said? *For it is better to suffer from the disease of life and die from it than not.* Poetry," sneered Albert. "That's their answer to everything." Albert shrugged and returned to the mirror. "*The disease of life.* What can you say to that?"

"Is there really not another room I can stay in?"

"Oh, he won't bother you—don't even worry about that. A part of me wishes they would just get rid of failed bachelors—I mean, really get rid of them. But then, I know, I know, who'll go on to the civil service. Still."

"Albert!" Ben and Albert jumped. Another bachelor joined them in the living room.

"Selfridge!" said Albert. "Selfridge, meet Ben."

Ben and Selfridge shook hands; Selfridge's hands were brutally huge and damp. One of the massive hands went to Selfridge's mouth; he picked absentmindedly at his chapped lips.

"Ben," he said.

"Selfridge."

"Selfridge is new to the house, too."

"Nice suit, Ben."

Albert clapped Ben on the back, "Leave the poor guy alone—tailor's still working on his suit."

"Huh. And what do you do, Ben?"

"Selfridge does guns," interrupted Albert.

"Does guns?"

"Guns," said Selfridge. "I collect them, draw them, fire them—you name it."

"Were you in the war?" asked Ben.

"You challenging me?"

"No, I was just asking—"

"No. Not in army. Understand? I'm more of a *connoisseur* than an enlisted type. And you, Ben. What's your game?"

"Um, I paint—I mean, paintings."

Selfridge seemed to regard him with sudden deep antipathy. The door to the Bachelor House swung open; bachelors were swarming out into the sunny yard. Selfridge turned to go and knocked a marble egg from the mantel to the floor, shattering it. He stepped over the wreckage and pushed his way into the crowded hallway.

"He broke the egg," said Albert sadly. "It wasn't mine, but still. I kind of liked it."

"It seemed like an accident," said Ben.

"Maybe."

Ben followed Albert out into the streets. Hundreds of bachelors were strolling in loose formation toward the park. Ben wanted only to go home, to go back to his little room and lie still in the little bed and think, think clearly. His life's work was opening up before him, and he felt nothing for it. It had seemed so effortless in the abstract! Now here he was.

Albert ran ahead to tackle Selfridge, and Selfridge hurled Albert into the hedges lining the street. Ben stooped to offer a hand as Albert struggled to free himself. "These are nasty little branches," he said, hairline scratches emerging across his face. "You go ahead. I'm good; I just need a minute to normify. I'll see you in the park."

"OK," said Ben. "But I'll be there later—need to check on my suit first."

When he reached the park gates, Ben drifted away from the other bachelors and headed for the river, soundless and flat, blanketed in a layer of cold, rank air. The water was toxic—rotten, despite its breadth and depth. Ben felt his heart swell with affection for it, for the putrid smell, the mix of algae and trash captured by the black rocks against the shore. How could he love this grim, dirty stretch of the river, its unpleasantly chilly and fetid atmosphere? Perhaps one day he would have the same affection for the peculiar, bad smell of this cheap black suit, grow sentimental at the sight of Bachelor Houses, long for the days of important difficulty . . . strange feelings, but associations that were ever after his, therefore his possessions, something to be prized, no matter how perversely. He had missed the pitch of the city at full power—the rumble trucks, the bird fights, the mood-shattering keen of the ferry horns on the river.

A boy and his father sat at the river's edge. The father took a cigarette from his shirt pocket while the boy searched under the loose river rocks. The boy found a broken oar—left over from the days when rowing leisure craft upon the water was still ordinary sport, before the conversion of the river into a Restricted Zone. It seemed that the farther out they pushed the Enemy, the more powerful they made his local forms. For each acre of the Enemy's Territory they seized, the Enemy seized an acre of the citizen's mind. The boy held the oar like a rifle and fired rounds at the opposite shore; the father watched, trails of smoke streaming from his nostrils.

Ben followed the river into the heart of the park, sunny and in bloom—but *here* was beauty and affection, beauty and affection of the most natural order . . . the beauty of the natural world, the only love that ends neither in envy nor in satisfaction.

Bachelors, fit and ubiquitous in their tailored pale suits, napped in the golden light beneath the broad-leafed trees, or else they read intently (or seemed to), in the green folding chairs of the park. Young people, drowsy in light and linen cloth, suffused with sun, their hearts peaceful and warm as stones in beds of dry, sunny straw, their lungs as spacious as the vibrant tree branches through which the wind pushed and pulled. *There was nothing to fear under the warm wheat sun. . . .* Bachelors salted hard-boiled eggs and bit into them; young women carved the little roasted chickens. Cucumber slices were cool and clean circles on their plates. The wind picked up, threatening a hat, and a perfect hand reached out lazily to pin the brim along the soft trim of cool park grass. The sunlight hit Ben's face and head, drunkening him with the sense of boundless time and energy.

Ben could see the massive metal head of Captain Meeks peering out over the treetops, and he could discern the shadowy forms of the lesser statues scattered throughout the park: the Founders, the minor martyrs and soldiers and settlers, some burnished and gleaming in the cool green light of the trees, others degraded by graffiti lewd and bewildering, some seated on rocks, contemplating the earth, others pushed into the leaves by the height of their pedestals, faces locked in a moment of perpetual discovery and disappointment. There were those on foot and those on horseback; those studying the midair, the mild weight of a sealed former fate upon their smooth brows; those armed with guns and swords; those dragging broken chains; those slumped in grief; those with tiny hands and feet, beseeching, their childlike palms turned up to the heavens, to the tree branches, to the gossipy stir of leaves in spring, the gossipy stir of leaves forever, forever in judgment of them. Would their trials never end? Who were they, anyway? The statues made Ben forget; they induced a special forgetfulness in the shape of the person they should force him to remember.

Ben watched the opening of picnic baskets—the emergence of apples, green and red, salted pistachios bundled in handkerchiefs, dusted planks of bread, plate-sized rounds of cheese excavated clumsily by bachelors under the barely concealed disapproval of the young women in their company. A few bachelors rested their heads in the laps of the young women, who were talking or reading books while distractedly smoothing the hair of the sleeping bachelors, all of whom bore expressions of such profound peace, Ben imagined they would lie unperturbed if ferocious little animals dropped from the trees and commenced gnawing through the soles of their shoes. Ben longed to be among them—soon, he *would* be among them. Perhaps it wouldn't be so complicated after all, and he must remain optimistic.

Ben found a small hill safely removed from a gang of rambunctious bachelors who were laughing and tackling each other and calling out filthily to women as they passed. Mostly ignored, Ben noted, but not entirely. He sat cross-legged in the grass, plucking blades and folding them along their vertical seams and flicking them absentmindedly just beyond his knees. He looked down and took note of his hands: not exactly the hands of a young man. Hands perhaps too frightening to lay upon another.

A serious-looking young woman sat nearby in the grass to eat her lunch. She was alone, he was alone. If only he weren't the prisoner of this cheap, dark suit, the things he might say to her. *For I wore the pale suit and the bees sought out your hair, drawn gently in by the smell of flowers sleeping.* . . . Then the things she might say to him. It was an ideal day for a picnic: the ground was green, the sky was blue, the sun was yellow, the flowers were full and pink.

The young woman glanced up at Ben; he smiled at her and then looked away. He was thinking of what to say. He watched the legs of a spider turn the dark grains of soil between shoots of grass. He was thinking of what to say next. He could hear the sound of birds rustling their wings in the branches of the park trees. Ben stood—she would ask about the black suit, and he could touch stoically on his loss, his grief, an excellent place to start: with the sympathies of a young woman.

"My grieving friend!" a voice boomed out; Ben jumped. "We couldn't help but notice your heartbreaking suit, Brother!" Ben tried to ignore the voice, but it was already too late. He was soon surrounded by Brothers of Mercy, three of them, scrubbed clean, shirtfronts pressed into unbreakable boards of cotton, the childish talcum smell of them.

"This isn't a good time," said Ben.

"Brother," sighed one, "I think it is a good time. Grief can't be postponed, put off until it's most convenient. We're only here to help you, to listen to your troubles. Tell us about your pain, Brother, your broken heart."

Ben watched as the young woman wrapped up her lunch hastily and hurried out of the park, back into the city.

"Brother, we can help you. What have you lost? A mother? A father? You're all alone in this world, aren't you?"

Ben shoved past them and walked toward a general milling in the heart of the park, and as if he had plunged back into a corridor of oxygen, he was calmed by the crowds now parting on either side of him. Married men in bright ties and light sweaters, policemen in uniform, laborers in their grays smocks . . . bachelors, bachelors, bachelors. He stopped. Where were the other men in black suits? Did no one else in this city have to mourn? He stepped off the path and settled again, a few feet back, in the grass. I am grieving too hard and too deeply, he thought.

Meeks

I woke up beside the statue of the Captain, the gun requisition forms folded neatly in my pocket, a bag of apples by my head. I had been dreaming about the man in the black jacket. I had last seen him at the hospital, on a night long, long ago, or so it seems, though the human mind is surely the weakest instrument available in the study of the passage of time. We were at the hospital. The lights were out throughout the city for a Vigilance Drill. The attending Brothers of Mercy carried their blue-hued medical lights through the ward. I had climbed into bed with my mother, and I cradled her head against my chest. Her arm was draped over my knees, her hand dangled over the edge of my leg. I could feel the damp heat of her skin and thought: I won't feel this much longer, and then . . . I will *never feel it again.* The air was still, my grief imprisoned somewhere in my brain. I waited rationally, coolly, for Mother to tell me where to find my inheritance. I pictured a locked metal box, ice-cold in the soft, blind earth of the park.

The man in the black jacket watched us. A devoted son soothes his ailing mother, while a person of some eminence or intimacy looks on—this scene repeated itself up and down the ward. The apparent normalcy of our quaint tableau enforced by the presence of the Brothers, the presence, fading, of my mother. I believed her death should mean everything to those who were witnessing it. Brothers glided past us like sharks in the blue light, as if drawing strength from the air without breathing it, turning their ancient resignation in my direction: As for your suffering, it's all been done before. The man in the black jacket leaned back in his chair, his face falling out of the circle of blue light in which Mother and I resided. He was silent, every now and then making marks in a notebook that he held open on his lap.

We stayed like that for hours; the Brothers sometimes paused at the foot of the bed with their blue lamps swinging from rusted metal handles. The man in the black jacket sketching, filling up the pages of his notebook. Mother and I, her dying, me grieving, waiting to grieve. The Brothers walked on, down the row of beds, soaking the crisp, white sheets in the blue light of the medical lanterns. I wondered when and how Mother would communicate the location of my inheritance with all of these people listening and watching. I knew she had provided for me, but I didn't know how to proceed toward these provisions without her there as my guide.

Mother, I whispered, where can I find what I need?

She pointed feebly toward the ceiling and tried to speak. I leaned in very close. *Him,* she finally managed. In Him.

Captain Meeks? I whispered, and Mother was silenced by a wave of pain. I watched the agony pass over her face and waited patiently for her to return. *Him,* she insisted after a few minutes and pointed to the ceiling again.

Not *him,* Mother, I said, meaning the man in the black jacket, but she had disappeared into another red wave of pain. I glanced at the man in the black jacket, hunched over his notepad in the low light, and felt confident that he was not the *him* in question. I wished that he would go, so that Mother and I could speak more openly. I stared thoughtfully at the ceiling, gazed into the blue light passing in waves across the rafters and imagined I was deep underwater: the wooden rafters were the keels of powerful ships bobbing on the surface, the lifeless bulbs were the silhouettes of eels and fish. I considered that I alone knew something about what my mother had endured in life but that I still knew almost nothing; a whole universe of unacknowledged suffering was about to disappear forever, its infinite wrongs to go eternally unrighted.

The man in the black jacket stood suddenly, and I saw him standing, as if headless, illumined only to the shoulders by a Brother's medical lantern. He and the Brother spoke in low tones.

It took eight Brothers to part me from my mother. The man in the black jacket remained by her bedside, staring silently, as if a screen had dropped between the world and him, and he saw nothing and heard nothing of the massive struggle under way. I wanted only to be with her until the very end, to absorb the sight of her once and for all. I fought and I shouted; I called out to my mother. She turned her head, delirious, as if I were chasing her in a dream. The man in the black jacket leaned in close to my mother; she was speaking, mumbling feverishly, as if she did not know her only son, would mistake this thief for her flesh and blood.

Don't say another word, Mother! Mother, do not speak another word!

Sunlight crept up the sides of the buildings along the grand avenue, their enormous shadows were cool, dark blue pools . . . inviting. I pressed my forehead against the park gate. I used to spend hours just like this, leaning against the bars of the gate, waiting for women to pass so that I could pretend to mistake them for my mother. I hadn't been on the grand avenue in many years, per Bedge's orders, but when I was young, Mother and I made the trip together once or twice. The man in the black jacket would take us, out of the park and into the wilderness. Throughout the city in those days, new buildings, both homely and spectacular, were springing up everywhere, all cut from the same gray rock, the strong, desirable stone mined from the Enemy's Territory. Who could imagine a world without buildings, regular as mountains, gray and brown, always frowning in the distance. But they were once rare and rarely seen, and one had to wade through a world dense with trees. The man in the black jacket dug in his pocket. He handed me one of the city mints, and he took one for himself. I popped the mint into my mouth, prepared for its unpleasantly medicinal taste; though I was a small boy, I had already acquired a taste for the city mints. Mother stood beside me, holding my hand.

The man in the black jacket pointed to an immense building still under construction and said, My masterpiece! I clicked the hard mint thoughtfully against my teeth. As we watched from the opposite side of the street, workers ascended their ropes. The man in the black jacket pointed here and there, explaining everything to my mother and me. Mother had already explained to me that there were people in this world who lived in the tiny houses crushed together on irregular plots, and there were the people with more staircases than they knew what to do with, and then there were people like us, who preferred to spend their lives outside. (As a girl, my mother had watched her own parents being crushed to death by the little house they had grown to love and trust.)

The man in the black jacket pointed toward the heavens. Watch this, he said. Dangling high above the street, the workers pulled on their thick leather gloves and attacked the rock with everything they had: chisels, drills, hammers.

These are just finishing touches, said the man in the black jacket contentedly.

Soon the building would glow with the mysterious light I often observed from the park. I imagined the smell of roasted meat drifting out past the workers and into the open sky as the building came to life beneath their hands; on a narrow table by the window, I pictured a man's crisp white handkerchief . . . imagined the gentle, water-soft scent of apples ripening in a bowl in the open air, then the racket of keys and coins thrown onto a little plate by the door. (When a man comes home, he empties his pockets onto a little plate.) I'm home! he shouts deep into the building, and then there are the happy sounds of human life. A woman's voice—very quiet, very LOUD, very quiet, very LOUD—makes the man laugh, or sometimes it makes his blood boil.

My heart swelled with longing for an intimate study of this kind of scene, for closer quartering with these elusive beings. I considered that these workers must be artists, artists who broke through relentlessly to the human happiness that was sleeping in the rock as honey sleeps beneath the pollen-dusted, warm bees, and through their work the buildings were converted from unremarkable gray blocks of stone into living things. I looked up at my mother.

These buildings are alive! I said. Like *trees*. She cut me an angry look and tightened her grip painfully on my hand. They are not at all like trees, she said sternly. Trees are living things. She knelt beside me and whispered into my ear, These buildings are graves, and these men *gravediggers*.

Mother, of course, made quite an impression on me.

As we walked back toward the park that day, the man in the black jacket and my mother talked about various construction techniques that he hoped to refine, others he hoped to eliminate entirely. We walked along the big bland avenue, smooth and cool in the shadows of the buildings. People coursed in and out of the buildings, and my chest tightened with fear for those who were about to go in, and

I sighed with relief for those who had just egressed . . . the undead, the walking dead, suddenly back on the crowded streets with us. I held my mother's hand and tried to imagine us entombed in one of the inside rooms—her chopping fruit on a piece of hardwood, me at the window shouting for help.

The man in the black jacket walked with us and spoke to my mother in low tones. I listened to my own thoughts, tried to memorize his smell: ghostly pipe smoke and sweet buttery soap. People nodded politely at him as we passed. Up and down the street, I noted configurations that resembled ours—children walking hand-in-hand with adults. I contemplated reaching out casually with my free hand to take the hand of the man in the black jacket, but just then, he shoved his hands deep into his pockets.

Why was my mother spending so much of her time—time we might have been spending together—with someone involved in such an unsavory enterprise, one of which she clearly disapproved?

When she returned from her afternoons with the man in the black jacket, usually bearing some little gift for me, some apples or a little knife or a warm scarf, she was given to solemn, distracted, almost mystical conversation. I gave her my full attention. I listened carefully, tried to glean the important lesson, but the less I understood, the more her voice seemed pure and urgent . . . the indisputable sound of my mother speaking to the universe and me, as if we were one and the same: *You will never suffer as I have suffered,* and she would take my hand in one of her broad, strong hands.

I was standing in front of the still-grand building, the man in the black jacket's masterpiece, and daydreaming about the past, when I realized that quite a few people had gathered and were eyeing me uncomfortably. I nodded reassuringly—I wasn't there to arrest anyone. Finally, I raised my voice: Disperse, disperse! But they stood and stared, and as they stared I felt an old pressure building in my brain. I heard the flutter of black wings, the spectators and I turned to look up the street: the Brothers of Mercy were coming. As sinless as children, they smelled like children, as they wrestled me effortlessly to the ground and then hoisted me into the air. I kicked and shouted, I screamed Bedge's name. They were hustling me toward the river as if I were an infected corpse from the Age of Plagues, and when we reached the city dump behind the old prison, they hurled me onto the garbage heap with all their strength and turned back toward the city, their black garments whipping in the wind, and then they were gone.

But I was soon surrounded again—a group of career garbagemen made their ominous circle around me.

Brothers, I said, watching them carefully as I sat up and made a show of straightening my policeman's cap. They stared, blew smoke. One of them stabbed his garbage-stabber absentmindedly into the earth. Another coughed violently into his collar, startling birds into the air. The sky was inking up with birds, clouds of black-winged birds, the low grumbling heavens, the oily silken rustling: I felt sick. General conditions can change without warning: in one moment, the world hangs in the brain, fond and familiar as a painting of one's own, and in the next, garbagemen rip you from your dreams and filthy birds are cutting the face of day with their vectors. I could hear a train in the distance, departing for the Sheds.

I'm a policeman, I said unsteadily, and stood, backing away from the garbagemen—so long as I stayed moving, however slowly, I wasn't in their jurisdiction, and they knew it.

The city dump, which I had never visited, was a revelation—I wandered the heaps of refuse, steering clear of the workers who were raking trash from pile to pile. What a wealth to be found! I found some fresh canvas with which to line my boots—I wondered if I might find the incomparable gold of new warm boots hidden in one of the piles.

But I was distracted by the unpleasant odor of the Brothers of Mercy, which was all over my jacket. I went to a hidden spot along the riverbank and dunked my jacket into the oil-slicked and scummy water that pooled between the rocks. I removed my jacket only when exchanging it for a new one, and it seemed to me I'd had this one for several years. I squeezed the black water from it then slapped it clumsily against a rock, just as I'd seen the laundrymen do, all of my life in the park.

Ben

He had spent the day with the tailor, consumed three pots of the old man's acrid, watery tea, eaten an entire tin of stale cookies, and grinned numbly through hours of ancient, endless, looping tales ("In those days, Ben, they called us clothmen . . .") only to lose his nerve when the tailor asked if there was anything he needed. "I'm fine," he'd said. "Doing well, thanks," and made a point of misbuttoning his black jacket, as if to politely contradict himself.

On his way back to the Bachelor House, Ben cut through the park, joining the evening drift of families headed for home, their frustrations domesticated by the sheer elemental force of a beautiful, perfect day. The shadows grew long; bachelors and young women hurried in the opposite direction, out for the night. He could smell the cologne and cedar soap of bachelors' best intentions; the women left him in a wake of cool perfume.

Ben climbed the stairs to his room, impatient to be free of the black suit, to fall across his narrow bed and sleep and sleep and sleep. He kicked off his boots and saw that the other bachelor's door was open—he froze in horror. He was probably bound by law to say hello. The gap between the door and frame glowed with obligating light, but he wanted only to lie down and to think—think clearly—about things. He crept past the door toward bed.

"Hello?" Snared! There's no escape from a friendly greeting. "Hello?" the voice said again.

The bachelor was sitting on the floor, his pale pants rolled up to his knees. He was painting his ankles with a fine-haired brush. On his left leg was a pair of old-fashioned ships carving through blue swells. The right leg was the site of a conflict between two armies, one massive and clumped on a ridge, the other undermanned and dispersed, scattering into the pine shadows to escape a hail of bullets. Ben recognized the famous battle immediately. The bachelor painted. Ben watched uncomfortably from the door. The bachelor's hair was uncivilized, his lips tannin-dark with wine (a bottle stood nearby). He was gaunt, intent; he shifted his gaze and stared at Ben.

Ben stared back, frowning slightly. The bachelor studied Ben's suit. "My mother," said Ben quickly.

"I'm very sorry," said the bachelor and put down his paintbrush.

"I'm Ben," said Ben.

"Finton," said Finton.

Ben laughed nervously. "They reassigned my mother's house while I was away, so . . ."

Finton's room was pleasantly dark, dark with hardwoods and two walls of old books. The window stood open, admitting the evening air. The drawings pinned on the far wall lifted occasionally in a breeze. Ben edged between Finton's bed and a piano that took up nearly a quarter of the room to study one of the drawings—a man despairing on a black island observed by three skeletal horses; the mast of a wrecked ship piercing the surface of the dark green sea.

"It's a self-portrait," said Finton. "Marooned, as it were."

Ben thought of his paintings across the hall. "I paint," he said apologetically.

"Really?"

"I guess I'm interested in repetition, not the epic sweep."

"It's all the same," said Finton.

"But these are so good you could work for the city."

"Why would I want to do that?"

The awkward silence descended again; Finton looked relaxed, almost bored. Ben rested a hand on the piano.

"Would you like me to play something?" asked Finton.

"I could listen to a short piece."

"Is that what you want?"

"Of course," said Ben, feeling trapped.

Finton directed him to the armchair in the opposite corner. The arms of the antique chair were of carved mahogany, the seat and back upholstered in rich green velvet. "This is nice," said Ben, taking a seat.

Finton bowed slightly. "It is yours to occupy any hour of the day."

Ben smiled shyly. It was an unbelievably comfortable chair. Finton began to play. The walls of the room had been painted a dark, deep green, Finton's drawings hung in gallery columns. The oiled-wood desk, Finton's neatly hanging sweater, his corduroy slippers, the stamped spines of his books. Ben started to feel better. The open window let in the evening breeze, the scent of rosemary and lavender growing in the window box came and went. Finton played one of the classical movements, music borne of the days that preceded them, the heartbreaking times that had preceded them, days so dense with tragedy that they might live five hundred of these easy years yet never understand.

Ben studied a photograph propped on the windowsill. Finton standing in a beautiful pale suit, his polished shoes smooth as black stones in the bright, short grass. Finton held a rifle casually in his right hand, the barrel angled at the green earth. Ben could see the shapes of other men in the background.

"Where's this?"

Finton continued to play. "Afternoon hunt. Listening Party."

"You've been to a Listening Party?"

"Last of the season. The very best."

"And you didn't . . . you didn't find a wife?"

"Nope."

Ben sat in worried silence. *Even a stone can find love at a Listening Party.* A man lucky enough to make the guest list might easily relax into the conviction that he was as good as married.

"Don't worry," said Finton. "I didn't want to meet anyone, but I'm sure you will."

Ben stared at the photograph, suddenly desired a change of subject. A pair of patrolling boots stood in the corner. "Were you a soldier?"

"Ancient history," said Finton. "So was my father,

and his father, and so on. I thought I'd learn something interesting."

"Me, too."

"All we ever did was play cards in the mud and make ourselves crazy, listening, listening, listening. . . ."

"Where were you?"

"Upper Ridge Patrol."

"Me, too. Like my father. But after Upper Ridge, he volunteered for Advance Coastal."

"Highest casualties."

"He went down with his ship."

"Fathers," said Finton, as if in disbelief, and shook his head.

"And did yours . . . ?"

"Come back? He did. And in exchange for his service, he was offered the vaunted post of Dog Inspector, for life. Uncomplaining to the end, he spent his final years in close communion with the balls of dogs, the best balls of the best dogs—policemen's dogs. Cheek and jowl!" said Finton and laughed, which struck Ben as inappropriate under the circumstances (the discussion of the memory of one's own father), but he was in no mood to argue with a new friend. He watched Finton's back as he played. One way or another, he would soon have a fine pale suit. He imagined himself standing in Finton's room, buttoning and unbuttoning a beautiful jacket. "What do you think?" he might ask. "Very sharp," Finton would answer sagely, looking up from one of his books.

The Father's Tale, Part 1

The world was once pure: animals tilted their perfectly formed heads to listen to the workings of the great clock, the churn of the crystalline waters over the sunlit rocks. All was well. Then a twig snapped. Something was coming. It was I. I was traveling in my characteristic way: lumbering, unstoppable, crashing through the fragile woods.

We had been on patrol all summer without encountering any sign of the enemy, much less the Enemy himself, and I had come almost to enjoy our missions along the Upper Ridge, from which we had command of the entire countryside, the broad black harbor fading into open sea at one end and contracting into the fat vein of the city port at the other. We marched in silence. I wandered among my own thoughts. I was thinking about the gloomy lane of old poplars that lead to my grandfather's house, the rusted iron pots that hung ominously from the ceiling—my senses took note of the contrasting lightness of our combat-issue tin cups, the clatter of them bouncing on our packs as we trudged along the ridge without stealth (another memory rescued by association!). If Ben has a son of his own one day, I'll take my turn at playing the wild-haired old man living in a shack outside the city, obsessing over the Enemy, hoarding food against the Enemy, sorting bullet casings in the pitch black of cabin night, waiting for the Enemy to come at last, just as my own grandfather did.

The river slogged far below us and out toward sea. To think that I had spent most of my life in the city gazing across the water to this very spot, contemplating the silhouettes of these major and then-distant trees: the tall pine shadows planted in ruthless lines long ago by the settlers—

those mysterious beloveds, those incomparable villains. *Who were they, who were they?*

"Ah, who are you talking to?" someone called out.

"*No one,*" I answered immediately.

"You looked like you were talking to someone," said my fellow soldier, smirking.

"Just thinking," I said. "You should try it sometime."

We lashed things more tightly to our packs and marched on—I went back to the life-saving slog of remembering. My father brought his father to our house every Sunday for dinner. My grandfather swore that his wife, my grandmother, whom he had always disdained as a "deep thinker," had chosen to retire early to the Sheds. My mother regarded him coldly, politely, as he spun his lies; she kept his glass full of the rancid gum liquor he loved, and he was soon fumigating my face with his tirades against the Enemy, whose men were "as lithe as cats" and whose women were "as brawny as men." He leered at me, listing in his chair: "Now, listen. This is serious. There you are—finger on the trigger—facing the Enemy. But, wait—what are you going to do? 'Cause, is it a man or a woman? What do you think?" I would stare silently into the food on my plate, brace myself for what the old menace would forge next in the furnace of his rotten mouth, into which he loved to shove the hot plum and cream my mother brought to him. "And, see, that's just it—why are you thinking? Don't think, Son. Just shoot it." I touched the handle of my knife, intending to kill him with it when I was bigger and stronger.

He had once shown me a stash of the Old Money, which he kept under the floorboards his cabin. "Just in case," he said and clamped his hand over my mouth. I could feel his callous palm against my lips, smell the pipe tobacco and old-fashioned soap on his fingers: "Keep our secret"—and I had. What a marvel . . . the massive pull of the continuity of civilized life.

The trail dipped lower into the dangerous valley; instinctively, I softened my footfall. All the native creatures of my brain (hopes, dreams, worries, expectations) crouched like hunted animals at the edge of a clearing. We marched in silence, listened.

Autumn came: the ground turned soft and gold in the sunlight; the trees were beautifully black and skeletal in the cold rain. Around a damp, smoky campfire, we helped each other to picture life in the city. Soldiers longed for holiday cake, for the spectacle of Independence Day, now, by our reckoning, under way. They made lewd wagers about the quality and quantity of young women still at large in the city.

But the longer I spent in the Enemy's Territory, the more I preferred to be alone, to sit quietly among the trees, awed by the beauty of the copper-black twigs against the powder-blue sky. At first, I attacked these unacceptable feelings with logic: the Enemy was trying to get a foothold in my thoughts. I reminded myself daily how much I detested his filthy customs, his sneaky nature, his simple-minded, worshipful attitude toward the trees, toward the animals of the world, an attitude that grants the unthinking routines of beasts something of a human characteristic. I reminded myself that the Enemy would love nothing more than to kick in the door of my family's house and murder us one by one, to shove aside our butchered bodies and take down the dinner plates, throw the cutlery into a heap on the table, raid our cupboards, tell his blood-weaned sons a long black lie about how *my* land and *my* city and *my* house had come to be theirs, the house they had stolen, the house in which they were now taking their ease and telling their tall tales, until the true story of my life was replaced by the Enemy's. My wife, our son, our life, our joys and sorrows . . . all of it forgotten, forever.

I hated the violence an enemy necessitated in my heart, when I felt that we were a people devoted to other people, to family life. When I opened my pack, I sometimes feared I would find my wife's head, sawed crudely from her body by the Enemy and snuck into my possession, as a way of destroying my mind. Or I feared I would stumble upon the body of my son, impaled on a broken branch along the ridge, or that I would wake to find that all of my fellow soldiers had been quietly knifed in their sleep.

I had always been able to summon scenes of incredible brutality effortlessly, and though I attributed these scenes to the Enemy, it struck me now that these scenes were entirely mine. In my daydreams, the Enemy thirsted for my blood, sacrificed his brothers, his sisters, his own children, in gruesome and ruthless military tactics—the unbelievable bloodlust of an enemy I had never seen. And an unseen enemy the mind must construct entirely from itself, from the raw material of its own desires and fantasies. I frightened myself.

Winter came. The earth was a white and flawless sheet: the muddy, rutted ground we had patrolled and patrolled suddenly pure, as if never trod upon. It was beautiful. I wandered into the immediate woods to be alone. I propped my rifle in the snow and sat upon an ice-cold rock to rest. The woods were still, bright, and silent—my mind wandered; like a man suddenly unchained from the wall of a prison yard, my mind set out full of life and hope in the direction of its own concerns. I sighed heavily in the winter air, watched the mist of my breath travel. Bright red berries thrived on the black limbs of the snow-capped trees. I tilted my head back to take in the startling heights of the evergreens.

Then I heard the devastating crunch of one of my fellow soldiers approaching. My stomach tightened; I was sick again. I lay my head against my knees in defeat, pretending to sleep; dutifully I chained my mind back to the prison-yard wall. I was sorry to do it, to be forever playing the villain in my own brain. I raised my head and nodded grimly at my friend. "Saw you wander off alone," he said kindly. "Thought I'd come over.

"This reminds me," he said settling down on a nearby rock, "of the story of the two brothers who went out to Crippler's Field to hunt." I confess I was stunned. He must worry that I'm seriously adrift of our mission, I thought, if he's hauling out this old corrective.

I kicked my boot heel against the rock and knocked free the pressed tread of snow. He said, "Do you know Crippler's Field—it's about an hour's walk from the train station, just beyond the city limit? It's where the good hunter died at the hands of his very own brother . . ." I nodded. He went on. Somewhere in the city was my dissatisfied little boy, wishing powerfully for sweets, for me—a boy presumably afflicted by that mix of the wishful and the indifferent so characteristic of the young.

One evening, we were crowded around a low fire on the overhunted ridge. In the cold silence of the wintry woods, we were telling each other familiar tales to pass the time. A light snow was coming down. Men who had families talked about their children. I sometimes talked about Ben in an obligatory way. "He's a good boy," I'd say in a voice that had become so dead and dispiriting I was amazed it passed muster with the other men. In truth, if I thought of my son that winter, I tended to remember him as a lazy, greedy animal who ate and slept, and then attacked me suddenly with questions: "What does it do, where does it come from, why is it crying, will it fit in my room?"

Of course I used to attack my own father in just the same way. There's a friendly pain that halts self-investigation—but it's only a matter of time before we discover that we can plumb the depths of one another and easily forget that pain in others. When my father came home from the war, he made a show of picking up his old pleasures to reassure us, but I could see that he was a changed and damaged man, and when other ideas got the better of him, he simply walked off to be alone until he could master his feelings. I trailed at a distance, tracking him through the woods. I considered that Ben might someday hunt me in the same way, catching my shadow moving among the trees, forever trying to please me, to see me, to keep me. I felt I would do almost anything to stop him from following me through life—

We heard an alien sound—the animal-expert footfall of an Enemy soldier moving through the ice-glazed darkness beyond our campfire. We stopped talking. We heaped the fire with snow, and we fanned out into the forest. My blood was pounding in my ears as I crept across the eerie luminescence of the snowfield alone.

From the dark ridge, I aimed my rifle into the woods—a cavern of tar-black air even in the moonlit night. Then I spotted them—my enemies crouched among the trees; I watched the white fog of breath leave the black silhouettes of their heads. God, why wouldn't they just leave us *alone,* let us live in peace? I could hear the boots of my commanding officer crunching stealthily through the snow, closer and closer. I knew what he would make me do. I decided to run. I hurried, unseen, down from the ridge and crept along the trampled path. I wanted to be left alone, and to leave others alone. All night I tried to make my way down the other side of the dark ridge, toward the water. I had noticed a ship anchored offshore that morning. Ours? Theirs? Something else entirely? I hardly cared—so long as I could be anywhere else, do anything else.

I woke the next morning in a cave of pines, feeling sick: I was a deserter, a coward. What if the Enemy had bided his time and then slaughtered my fellow soldiers in their sleep, because I had not named him, not called him out? I had fled from the faintest suggestion of the Enemy—his black silhouette, his white phantom breath.

I climbed back up the steep slope of the ridge to survey my position. I found the harbor and could see more clearly the mysterious ship upon which I had pinned all my hopes—burned out and sunk in the rocky shallows.

A branch snapped. I spun around, terrified, and aimed my rifle into the trees, but I soon saw that it was only a wild horse regarding me coldly from between the snowy pines of the ridge. I lowered my gun. As if carved from gray ice, as if made of stone and dusted in snow, a ghost horse with black eyes. The horse and I stared at one another, both stock-still. I was thinking only of myself, of my broken heart. I could have regarded this unlikely creature either as a messenger of good tidings or as my enemy, and I felt sorry for myself, because I had thought of him immediately and deeply as an enemy of mine.

I said, "Fine! You win," and I threw my camp knife, and it landed near the roots of a pine tree; and I threw my rifle, and it sank into the deep snow. Then I longed for the thin illusion of life that I had always taken to be Life to be displaced by the brutal, enormous, beautiful certainty of something greater, even if I were destroyed in the process. I waited. Nothing happened. The horse sighed, scraped at the snow with his pitch-black hoof.

There was nothing to do now but return to what I had always known and hope that what I had always known had survived the night.

I trudged along the ridge until I reached camp—I whistled a much-loved bit of triumphal music along the way; I displayed my empty hands high overhead lest I be shot by the boy from Crippler's Field or any of the other boys.

"I saw a horse," I told the commanding officer as I warmed up later beside the low fire crackling in the gray light of the afternoon.

"That's it? That's all you saw?"

"That's it."

"But how did you lose your rifle?"

"I fell," I said, "down an embankment. I couldn't find it again in the snow."

"You're lucky to be alive. Where's your camp knife?"

I looked searchingly around the camp. "It's here some-where," I said and shrugged.

The commanding officer studied me. "Are you all right, Son?"

"Just cold," I said.

"Buddy, give him your pistol."

Buddy gave me an assessing look—who was I, and why

was he always paying for the stupidity of others? He growled at me under his breath and slapped the pistol into my open palm.

JULY

The sea is full of life, indifferent to men,
Just as the brown legs of the horses seem to pump infinitely—
Until they are thrown upon the sun.
Young Man, lay that precious, pounding heart
of yours upon the table, and see it for what it is:
A thing that dies in autumn.

Ben

"Shouldn't you be out on the town, hanging around people your own age, meeting young women?"

Ben sat slumped in the infernally hot front window of the tailor's shop. "In this?" he said, and tugged at the wilted, black lapels of his suit.

"Ben," warned the tailor.

Ben watched the butcher working in his shop across the street; he had been gazing into an empty display case for what seemed like hours. Maybe if Ben could emanate private pain through a layer of stoic, cool-headed conversation, the tailor's mind would shift sympathetically in his direction. "I'm sorry," said Ben. "You're right."

"Why don't you try to get a suit from the Brothers of Mercy?"

"Then I might as well not bother! I might as well turn myself over to them now. I'd owe them my life."

"You'd rather owe me."

"One suit won't ruin you."

"Ben, I mean it."

"Why can't you make an exception?"

The tailor was cutting squares of fabric into smaller squares. "Every last one of you thinks of yourself as the special case. It's interesting to me how everyone pleads the special case using such generic terms. You all feel entitled to whatever you want in life, and each of you seems to think that your suffering is beyond compare. And beyond that, you don't think. I've heard it all, Ben. And the days of special dispensations are over. You are not a boy. You are a grown man. I'm sorry things aren't turning out as you had hoped."

"You'd make an exception for your son," Ben said peevishly.

The tailor gave Ben a long look. "Of course I would, Ben. What father wouldn't? Your mother, a woman of infinite kindness and optimism, had such high hopes for you. She thought you might do well in life. And then you enlisted, of all things. Always hot on the heels of your father," said the tailor, mocking Ben's tone. "All your mother wanted was for you to find happiness in life, to marry well, to have a family that would fill up the rooms of the old house. I cared for her a great deal, Ben, but I'll tell you this right now. You mention the suit again, and I'll throw you out of this shop for good. Now, I'm tired of watching you sulk. It's a beautiful day—you should be outside. And don't come back until you've cheered up. I hope you're not glowering at young women the way you're glowering at me. Try looking a little happier."

"I have nothing to be happy about! Besides, it's not a beautiful day. It's hot and everyone's miserable."

"Well. You're unlikely to meet anyone with that attitude—you'd be amazed what a positive outlook can accomplish. Consider the difference between that shop"—the tailor nodded toward the butcher—"and this one. As the adage goes, 'A boy may thrive, while his brother fails.' In the story, Ben, they've shared every advantage, yet one permits failure to enter his life, while the other doesn't."

"Yes, thank you," said Ben. "I am aware of the story and what it means."

Ben walked through the park, frowning at women—when he walked, he thought, and when he thought, he frowned; it couldn't be helped. And what if the tailor was wrong, what if forcing a good attitude dulled the blades of thought, softened and corroded the mind so it could prepare itself for less and less?

He passed the police station and paused to study the tattered posters pasted along the south wall: happily married couples walking by the river; children laughing through mouthfuls of cake (disgusting); young men in pale suits, shotguns tipped jauntily over their shoulders; gray workers turning vague and massive cranks in the shadows. The Consequences of Failure! Duly noted: the official exhortation to pursue one's own happiness or be put to the task of generating happiness for others, or worse—to be not in the picture. Had he accomplished anything? Ben thought of all the pointless visits to the tailor, the hours spent fending off the Brothers' efforts to administer mercy in the park, the merciless sarcasms of other bachelors, his own ham-handed attempts at conversation with young women. He had to reach so far back to lay his hands upon a truly happy memory. What if he was becoming, or had become, an unlovable man? What if the toxin of failure was already coursing through his veins, what if he was already stinking of defeat? *Women sense things, know you before you know yourself . . .* The tailor was right—he had to think differently, or else his brain would cloud over permanently, and his poor heart would have to chug the cold, dirty blood until it stopped.

Perhaps these unhappy scenes were the raw material of lasting happiness, as was often the case in stories. In the old stories, future happiness was almost always directly proportionate to the amount of suffering that preceded it. In which case, Ben could expect a beautiful life, an excellent and happy outcome. Happiness being the final product of the machinery that was, for the moment, generating such unhappiness. Unhappy life scenes: where else could they land him except in the arms of another?

Ben yanked a cluster of pink flowers from a park tree; he tucked the blossoms into the buttonholes of his dark jacket and strode up the slope of the bachelors' hill, his heart beating fast, he felt faint with excitement. There were the hard black lines of the tree branches veining the pale blue sky; the streetlamps sentinel and straight beside the path. The green leaves shuddering in the occasional breeze. A perfect scene, a green globe of healthy activity, something of which he could simply elect to be a part. Ben made it across the bachelors' hill without incident, and he continued on to the park café, digging in his coat pocket for the few coins he had left.

At the café counter, a father lifted his young daughter so she could see the pastries on display, and the mother pointed to this one, then that one, calling each by name. The girl looked over at Ben, and then the father looked, too. Ben smiled and stepped back slightly, mindful of the unpleasant smell of his suit. The café owner stood by, his musty, eternally damp rag in hand. The girl pointed to a slice of cake on a small white plate.

Ben looked longingly at the sugar-powdered ring cookies and the slices of white cake, trying to choose. He thought of Independence Day: the autumnal chill, the blazing leaves, when he would lie beside his wife beneath the great tree.

The girl and her parents settled at one of the marble-topped tables. The father dug through the sugar bowl with his spoon, plowing beneath the surface, digging for virgin layers; he sugared his tea, then dropped the spoon noisily on the tabletop. He reached over and pinched a bite of cake from his daughter's plate.

The woman behind the counter watched Ben expectantly; the café owner shifted the musty rag from one hand to the other. Ben decided: cake. His last coins converted (effortlessly!) into an old, respectable pleasure.

Ben stacked his coins on the top of the glass case. "White cake, please."

The woman glanced at the café owner; the café owner tightened his grip on the musty rag.

"Been away?"

"Pardon me?"

"Because that," she said, pointing to the stack of coins, "won't buy you a slice of white cake. Not since olden days."

Ben noticed the postcards leaning against the counter—sentimental photos of boys in short pants running hoops down the street.

Ben's face was hot. "A cookie then."

"Have a mint," she said, and slid the bland bowl across the counter. Ben took a fistful of the mints—the city mints he hated.

He retreated to a park bench and threw the handful of mints into the grass. He looked down at his suit: the pink flowers in his buttonholes were ridiculous, he was a fool. He plucked the flowers out and threw them down. At this rate, he might as well grieve forever—his sadness cauliflowering into a mind that split into florets under the slightest pressure.

He watched bachelors walking between the trees hand in hand with young women. He saw Selfridge intercepting women easily on the path. A young woman approached. Selfridge stood in her way. Perhaps they were friends; they clearly knew one another, but maybe he had also *befriended* her? Ben pressed his palms against his eyes and pretended to massage them. He couldn't even get his body into the most basic pale suit. He imagined clinging to the young woman, her warm, clean form, her mind disconcertingly alert to hidden things. *God, please don't leave me here!*

On the other side of the bachelors' hill, families were enjoying the day. Children swung between their parents' hands. Fathers were decked out in kind and modest sweaters. Men on the other side of the great divide, men who had made it, men who had seen the beacon and plunged, and who had made it. And now they idled justly in their summer sweaters, and there were children who worried about them and women who worried about them and who, behind closed doors, comforted them as if they were boys.

That evening, Ben sat in the green chair in Finton's room, his shirtsleeves rolled past his elbows; his suit jacket hung in the dark of his own room across the hall. He tried to put the hated garment out of his mind. Finton sat at his desk, sketching languidly. Ben sipped tea in the heat and watched Finton work, as had become their routine.

"What are you drawing?" Ben asked to break up a long silence.

"The park," said Finton and held the drawing so Ben could see it. A crowd transfixed by the closed curtains of the Independence Day stage, while peach-colored flames devoured the city behind them. "The more hidden something is, the holier," said Finton. He studied Ben's face and added, "You know, this is my mother's house."

"What?"

"This is my mother's house, just as your mother's house was once your mother's house and, I would wager, is still, to you, your mother's house."

"But where is your mother?"

"Well, not here, obviously. They evicted her," he said, "when I was away. Just like you. They moved her out to the Sheds. I'm sure she's deceased by now."

"But, how are you even here?"

"I moved in slyly—became just like any other bachelor moving into a Bachelor House."

"No one knows?"

"Just you. If only I had married, et cetera, et cetera. A set of potentials with which you are familiar." Finton sighed. "That was Mother's favorite chair."

Ben scanned the room uncomfortably and reached for his tea, cold and ash-gray.

"What are you going to do?"

"Take it back."

"How?"

"Somehow."

"You'll go to prison, Finton. Or much worse."

"There's nothing worse than this, Ben. That's how they frighten you, they frighten you into believing there's something *even* worse. They let you enjoy the illusion: a bachelor king lazily shopping for his kingdom in the sunshine, master of all he surveys. But he has no subjects, no land, no courtiers, no enemies. *Aha!* The perfect human being."

Meeks

The days were dipping lower and lower into the cauldron. They were hot and long, and I was making nothing out of them. I was wasting the precious life given to me by my mother. The squirrels were taking their tiny, vicious bites of bland acorns; the beetles packed their lantern jaws with sour grass; the people were commiserating in the heat, longing for the copper hammer of autumn to strike their brains with crisp, sharp blows.

I slept very little; I ate almost nothing. The black fields of my brain were growing only one thing: I dreamed the shape of the man in the black jacket everywhere I looked . . . in the shadows under the noonday trees, in the mysterious shapes abroad in the fog, and it seemed to me, increasingly, that the city was an elaborate machine designed only to drain all the pleasure from my life.

I still made my rounds, though they often took me the entire day to complete, and I spent long hours sitting near the café waiting for the man in the black jacket to return to his old haunt. Families colonized the café tables and smiled benefactorially over the park—such pleasure in one's self, such pleasure in a world that lays itself down before one's senses. Men and women ordered cookies and slices of cake, and wheresoever they pointed, their wishes were fulfilled, and they fell into reverent silence as they ate, their minds bitten by the soft, sugary nips of memory—*Things are just as they've always been, let us be thankful*—each sweet bite is like a sacrament, a little portal easily pried open with a fork, a hole through which one can squeeze one's senses and return to the days of hope and innocence and excitement and fear. A pack of boisterous bachelors, their pale jackets bristling with flowers, their cufflinks throwing off sparks of sunlight, tried to take an empty table and were chased off by the café owner, wielding his wet-headed mop like a lit torch.

Here are all these people, these men and women, I thought—laughing and playing and gossiping and napping while they are up to their chins in dangerous golden light. Time is running out! They eat cake in the sun, and in the evening they drift away from the heterogeneity of one another's company, sated, and pass back through their own doors into private realms, realms as separate and diverse as distant planets, some cruelly small and over-furnaced, others jollily huge, regally cold, where on the verge of sleep, worries and fantasies bloom on that dusky, curved horizon that is the common seam, though I myself have never passed peacefully or wittingly across it, and I fear I may not always succeed in keeping distinct my rigorous empiricism from certain kinds of dreams.

They pretend at contentment, but I can hear the men and women deep inside their houses, culminating in the dark, the workers pounding down old complaints late into the night. The shoemakers hammering guiltily, *tink, tink, tink,* and gossiping, their dark, wet mouths prickly with black nails, their breath steaming the night air without clouds of antimony. But where is the source of this endless dissatisfaction? *What* is it? What's wrong with the human being who can't find happiness even in a world engineered to supply his every pleasure?

A man banged away at an empty ash bucket with two sticks; girls screamed—in happiness or in fear? I can never tell. All these *people.* The way they judge and congratulate each another (stranger to stranger) with a glance, the way they share, telepathically, their love of new sweaters in autumn, their love of public half-naps under the full summer sun, or the way they grin lamely at the children of others: I've got some! Or else, I want some! And the children are so energetic and delicate, these eager and fragile deputies sadly not yet privy to the larger scheme in which they will do their work.

To think that I've spent my life as a student of their Words, overheard, and that I had come to believe that a conversation between two people was the most complicated project in the known universe. *Hello* may be a blunt instrument, a common tool, but it cracks open worlds. All we've ever known, wanted, or felt floats into view, only to be scrapped by the *How are you?* How do human beings, so full of fear, so miserly of vocabulary, carry on?

"Like two sailors in a barrel," joked a bachelor from the grass, watching two civil servants pass, one helping the other to walk.

Even after the café had closed, I stayed, sat docilely through an evening rain. I was too heavy-hearted to move. My clothes were soaked, and water formed rivulets along the backs of my hands and trailed off each fingertip in a stream. The park path was empty and gray, the details crushed and clumped by the dusk and rainy weather.

The evening bells began to sound, echoing in the valleys between the buildings and thundering through the open spaces of the park. I sensed the old shadow falling across my brain, the slow bubbling-in of the black ink. A light fog seeped through the trees from across the river. The last of the bells fell silent. Mother had always said that all that was hers was mine.

A branch cracked and fell to the grass. Flowers still clung to it. I noted the gradations of yellow, the resiliency of the petals in the rain, the fine silver veins of the dark branch. I struggled, in the failing light, against the tendency of objects (the petals, the wet leaves, the trees in the distance, the gravel of the path) to fuse into large, vague shapes at night, but I knew the air would soon be black with them. I closed my eyes and tilted my face into the evening rain. I granulated and granulated the memory of the yellow flowers on the little branch, and soon I could see everything clearly: the soft green marrow of the snapped limb, the tiny imperfections along the edges of the petals. It wasn't thinking; it was a kind of sleep.

Ben

Life would be so simple if this were life, thought Ben. It would be very sweet if it were enough. Finton was sitting on the buckled hardwood floor in the kitchen, the broad oak planks flecked with paint from the annual repaintings of the kitchen walls, which soaked up the cooking of bachelor meals and the yellowish smoke of bachelors smoking. Finton was settling a young pepper plant in an ash bucket filled with the good, damp soil from the park. A rainstorm had come out of nowhere, cooling the air, tapping peacefully against the windows, filling the house with beautiful blue-gray light.

Finton was telling a long story while he packed earth around the pepper roots, and he was laughing at certain parts of the story, and he looked happy and relaxed, uncharacteristically healthy in the nice light of the storm. Ben was cutting up a tomato from the back garden to have with their toast, and he wished the other bachelors would never come home. They were out there somewhere, striving, hurrying, searching. Why not just live in the world one already inhabits, rather than pining and planning endlessly for the next?

If the world could freeze in a state of warmth, the birds to stop, to turn to father-smelling soap in the waxen green tree-tops; for the trees to stop pumping life to their extremities, to allow the soft green buds to stop, stay folded, sweet.

"Autumn was coming," said Finton. It was part of his story.

Ben heard the front door bang open, the unmistakable sound of Selfridge dropping his enormous boots in the hall. Finton flinched and stopped telling his story; Ben suddenly couldn't even remember what it had been about. Finton stood, brushing dark soil from his pants. *Would they never have peace?* Tears were welling up deep inside Ben's body, mercifully far from the surface of his face. He closed his eyes.

"See you later," said Finton.

Ben listened to Finton climb the hollow steps overhead. He picked up the little paring knife and stared at the tomato.

"Ben!"

"Selfridge."

"It's pouring out there!"

"Yes, big storm."

"Fists!" Selfridge barked and fell into a boxing stance.

"Not now, Selfridge."

"Fine."

Selfridge tugged at the sleeves of his pale suit as if concealing something—Was he wearing Ben's honeybee cufflinks again? His gold cufflinks that were a gift from his mother's father? Ben frowned and turned all of his attention back to the slicing of the tomato.

Selfridge stood closer; Ben could smell his tobacco sweat, his gardenia cologne tinged with gunpowder, the rancid wine on his breath. "Ben," he said, "I'm a little worried, buddy. What have you got going on here? You've missed out on yet another day. More importantly, you've missed out on many, many nice young ladies. Ladies abounded: forgiving ladies, Ben. You would have liked them. One young lady in particular. But what do you care—you've got your little tomato there, you've got your paintings, your pepper plant, your boyfriend, Finton."

"Shut up, Selfridge."

Selfridge sighed. "Ben's life."

Ben pointed at the pepper plant with his knife. "That's not even mine." Selfridge shook his head in disgust.

"Yes, one young lady in particular who likes Selfridge's hat and touched the brim with her hand. Here," he said, touching the brim of his hat, "and here," he said, touching it again. "I say this out of brotherly love, but if you don't get it together, get a proper suit, for God's sake, it's over."

"It's complicated, Selfridge . . ."

"Whatever. Instantly bored. Your old Selfridge won't be around much longer anyway."

The front door opened and slammed shut again. Albert dropped his boots in the hall and joined them in the kitchen.

"It's pouring out there!"

"Big storm," Selfridge said. "Albert, have you seen my snub-nose revolver?"

"Seriously, look at me—I'm soaking wet."

"Albert," said Selfridge sternly. "Concentrate on the words I'm speaking. Did you take my favorite?"

"Which one's that?"

"Adeline."

"Adeline?"

"Adeline the Snuggler."

"Ah, the Snuggler . . ."

"Albert, did you take Adeline?"

Albert opened his jacket, turned his pockets out, pouring water out onto the floor. "No, of course not, Selfridge. I'd never."

Selfridge turned to face Ben. "Ben?"

"What would I want with your gun?"

"I shudder to think."

"I paint, remember?"

"Ben. No more games. What have you done with Adeline?"

"I didn't take it."

"Her. We call it her."

"I don't have your gun, Selfridge. I don't know where it—"

"She!"

"Selfridge."

"Ben."

"Planning to get your suit from the tailor at gunpoint? You'd probably shoot the man in the face just to avoid an awkward conversation."

"No, he'd shoot himself, to be more polite," Albert said, squeezing rainwater from his sleeves.

Ben threw the knife into the sink, a faint, pathetic *clink*. "Shut up. Both of you."

Selfridge leaned closer. "I still say you're a death-by-attrition variation on the doomed-no-matter-what theme. Where's Adeline, Ben?"

Ben reached under his jacket. He slapped the revolver down onto the kitchen table.

"The Snuggler—easy to love, easy to lose. Explain yourself, you rotten thief."

"You took my honeybee cufflinks—fair's fair. You got it back—"

"Her."

"—now give them back."

Selfridge hitched his jacket sleeves, so Ben could see the honeybee cufflinks gleaming; he pointed the gun at Ben's face. "I don't shoot you right now, Ben, only because a particular young lady liked my *hat* and would like to walk in the park again this evening."

"That's enough. Come on, Ben," said Albert and held out his hand. Ben took it. Albert led him up the stairs and into the safety of his stiflingly hot room.

"Can't you open your window?" asked Ben. Albert dismissed the window with a wave of his hand, "It won't open. It's stuck, I think."

"Mine, too," said Ben. He saw that Albert had been packing: cramming badly folded clothes into the corners of his suitcase.

"What's going on?"

"I have some news: I've found someone," said Albert, and looked dazed. "We've reached an Agreement; I'm moving in tomorrow."

"So far ahead of Independence Day?" asked Ben.

"It's not that far," said Albert.

"Oh, come on," said Ben, "it's still pretty far."

They both jumped at the *pop-pop-pop* of Selfridge firing Adeline out his bedroom window and into the yard.

"I wish he wouldn't do that," said Ben.

Albert nodded. "Anyway, she and I'll live together for the rest of the summer, which isn't long, and then on Independence Day, we'll just officialize things."

Ben steadied himself by leaning on the windowsill.

"Selfridge and I are going out tonight to celebrate—you have to join us. Brothers! Bachelors!"

"I don't know. I should probably get some work done,

have to see the tailor early tomorrow morning . . ."

Albert's face brightened. "Is your suit ready?"

"Almost."

"Then you've got something to celebrate, too."

Ben and Selfridge waited in the living room for Albert to come down. Ben was studying a pair of patrolling boots propped against the back wall of the cold fireplace and thinking back over summer marches down the long forest lanes, evening copper light, sea air, the sound of waves crashing on the shore far below the ridge.

"Ben!" Selfridge hurled his pen at Ben's head. "Would you please shut up. I'm trying to write something."

"I didn't say anything."

"You're breathing like a bear. I'm trying to write a letter, a rhyming letter, for a woman. Throw me my pen."

"You're writing a poem?"

"No, Ben. We don't say 'poem.' Poetry is known world-wide as the sad sound of failure, as I'm sure you're well aware. I'm writing a rhyming letter."

They could hear Albert galloping down the stairs. He appeared in the door.

"Selfridge is writing a poem," said Ben matter-of-factly.

Albert raised his eyebrows. "*Reeeally?*"

"Ah, forget it," said Selfridge and tossed the paper to the floor. Ben read it as he walked over it toward the door. *Dear dear.*

A Brother's Tale, Part 2

You may have been wondering: *How does a gifted artist with a gentle nature turn to building bombs and dreaming of the wholesale destruction of his homeland?*

I'll tell you.

One afternoon, my brother came home and announced his engagement to our neighbor's daughter. Needless to say, Mother was beside herself. She shouted with joy and relief and exultation, burning through all that was fashionably said on such an occasion and then moving on to exclamations whose vintage had not been heard since the earth cracked open and gave birth to the mountain ranges. I had to listen to all of it as I lay on the floor of the front room.

"Where's my little brother?"

"Oh, who knows," I heard my mother answer, when, in fact, I had lain on the floor in the sun of the front room all day, and she knew perfectly well where I was. I stayed there.

Though I could sense the black shadow of the great bird of heartbreak gliding across open country toward me, I was still pretending that my brother's change of fortune was a game he and I were playing, and the next day, I followed him to the park, tracking him from the shadows, gleefully planning to tackle him against the bachelors' hill—when I saw him run into the arms of his fiancée and spin her in a circle. I was stunned. He took her hand, and they started down the main path, airing out their good fortune, nodding slyly at the people who were like them. I followed. I am not a stealthy man to begin with, and I was making no special effort to move like a cat, and yet they seemed not to see me. Perhaps they were blinded by joy—*my brother! my sister!*—unable to recognize the deformed animal stumbling through the garbage-laced gloom as one of their own kind.

The broad-winged shadow glided into the park, darkening the treetops, and raced down the western slope of my brain and directly into my heart: I collapsed to the grass and rolled onto my back and tried to breathe. My brother was as good as gone, lost to some stranger, to a life of soft summer blankets, to weekend picnics, to roasted chickens, rounds of cheese, mild green pears, tins of roasted nuts, salads, dried fruit, pastries, cakes, cookies. Is that what my brother had really wanted? To be ordinary, to spend his days going soft, entombed in comfortable rooms, listening deadfaced to the endless narrations of the large and small creatures around him? To be a family man?

I had snuck a bottle from my mother's house. I pulled it from my inside pocket and took a long, discreet drink, which immediately brightened my view of things and, not for the first time, saved my mother's youngest son's brain from obliterating despair.

It wasn't long before the sun sank into the river and people packed up their things and left in droves, and I had drunk most of the bottle and the park lights were giving off their cold, dazzling drunken penumbras, and I was alone, in every sense of the word. I wanted to climb onto the stage, something that was strictly forbidden, but I knew it was the only place on earth I could be happy. *If it's what you really want. . . .* I hesitated, fond as I was of the Old Counselor. He lived in my brain, but then so did Mother—her dreams, her dread, her sense of shame, they all tripped over each other in the effort to make me afraid of everything I wanted to try in life. All of *her* thoughts somehow living in *my* head. I drank until they drowned, and I climbed onto the stage, where it was easy to look out at the world with love. *See the tree-lined infinitude of the park! See the pale gravel paths that disappear into the black silences between the trees, which is Death, yet I fear it not!*

I saw two men struggling to carry a third man deeper into the darkness of the park, and I laughed freely at the comedy that derives, inevitably, from men trying to capture and carry unwilling objects.

I looked overhead and could see the ghostly tendrils of old rope that still hung from the high branches. I studied the old proscenium: the fog-streaked trees, the slate-blue river, the ships huffing blandly across the black harbor. The ships that had carried the men and women who killed every bird, leaf, frog, bear, and snake they found by naming it. The smile (it was a stupid grin) faded from my jolly sweat-slicked face, and I sank into an oil-black melancholy that I must have loved . . . since I sought it out so often. "And, lo, the ships begot the people," I declaimed, "and then more ships begot *more* people."

I hurled my empty bottle from the stage and heard it shatter against the hard brown fact of trees in the dark, and I saw the shadow of the park bum crouch and run. Always listening. I sighed, took comfort in the comfort that was there for the taking: I was a better man than some men, than at least one man. (Things could always be worse.) But an artist's job doesn't stop there, and just as I often tried to think of my oblivious, materialistic, self-absorbed fellow citizens as my brothers and sisters and to love them, I tried now to love and to find room in my heart for this foreign creature, and I reached an open hand toward the full darkness of the park, and I said, "My *brother* . . . remember me!"

Then I thought of the cold indifference of my real brother. If only I could obliterate once and for all the part of me that needed other people, I might become (through pain) an actor so great that I could lord over some part of the real world, even after death.

I turned back to the proscenium. I rocked back on my heels, I shoved my hands deep into the pockets, I leaned forward, and I charged it with all my strength, slamming my head clean through. I henched that ornamentation like a pro, busted it wide open, and my head, even in the swell of alcohol, burned with pain. I reeled backward, stunned, and put my hands instinctively to my head. I felt that it was slicked with blood, and to my surprise, vomit shot from my throat, and I fell facedown on the stage. I had struck the proscenium at the worst possible angle. My heart was beating frantically in my chest, and I detected—perhaps for the first time in my life—the eerie certainty of death living somewhere in my brain. In the excitement of what I had done (an extraordinary self-infliction), I saw very clearly just how far I had drifted from other people: no one would find me high up on the forbidden stage, and I would surely die, and die alone, a little tragedy that would be forever alloyed to my mother's joy over her other son, illuminating her pride with the shining gilt work of her grief.

The picture of the world was flickering in and out, and I crawled to the front of the stage, my hands wet and red, and I was full of alien feeling—it was terror, terror at the edge of my life. I wanted to be a different man, or at least remembered as a different man, and I cried out from the stage, from the full depth of my being:

'Tis true I hath head-punched the proscenium!
Forgive me, I was drunken when I hath done it.

I came to the next day, still prone on the boards, rough against my cheek, and my first thought, despite the severity of my condition, was of the beauty of the smell of the wood.

My body had only pain in it (it seemed to be made of pain), and yet I was newly attached to it: I was clinging to this world again, a weak and fearful little man in a blood-flecked pale suit. I heard the taut ropes and metal grommets go *tick, tick* against the flagpoles as the wind picked up in gusts that smelled like the river, and I could hear the broad-winged seabirds calling out to one another.

Later, I woke again to the smell of the Brothers of Mercy, their telltale stink, their talcumy sweat, and I retched, convulsing and coughing up rotten air. I could hear my brother's voice—*No, no, no!*—and I managed to open my eyes, and I could see the silhouettes of four or five Brothers standing around me, and I moved my hand, which seemed to weigh a thousand pounds, to cover what I imagined to be a frightening wound. My eyes rolled stubbornly back into my head, into the blackness of my brain, and I strained to see, and I could see that one of the Brothers was holding a gray workman's smock—*No, no, no!*—and my eyes rolled back again, and I thought, I've got to think carefully about what's happening to me. I heard my brother arguing. I heard him try to take the gray smock from the Brother's hands, and then I lost him again beneath the piles of black powder accumulating in my head. Distantly, I could hear the shouts of children filling up the park, and I could hear the fountain filling, eternally.

I woke in a small, dim room, on a bed of old coats. It took me a moment to perceive the other shape. My brother was sitting nearby in a wooden chair, his beautiful pale suit replaced by the gray workman's smock. There was an empty bottle on the table beside him. Until that moment, I had lived a blameless, worthless life. Now I had made something happen—something terrible, of course.

"They took Mother to the Sheds this morning," my brother said at last.

I covered my face with the coarse sleeve of my gray smock, in order to conceal from my brother any happiness that might appear, involuntarily, on my face. My brother and I were together again. Our mother was gone; my acting career was over; my brother's life was ruined, the love of his life probably weeping in the sun-streamed kitchen of her parents' house . . . who cares.

Our little room, our heart of hearts.

Ben

Ben was back in the old armchair in the tailor's window . . . watching the butcher, gulping down cups of the tailor's weak tea. He was sweating in the hot window, in the dark suit, his brain still congested with stale alcohol, with the memories and effects of a bachelor night. The tailor shuffled back to his worktable.

"I went out with some of the bachelors last night," said Ben, hoping to impress the tailor with news of his progress toward the norms.

"Are you planning to marry one of them?" asked the tailor. "Don't waste your time with other bachelors! Spend your evenings with *young women.*"

To think his fate was in this old man's hands, to think that an incapacitating grief over the loss of one man, the tailor's son, could so easily cause the death of another. And who would grieve for Ben? Albert? Finton? Ben folded a scrap of fabric thoughtfully and watched the butcher across the street pacing in his empty shop, the interior suffused with dim purplish light. Four or five grayish cuts of meat were stretched out under the bright bulbs of the display case. The butcher pulled a gristly plank of meat from the case and dropped it onto the chopping block to hack at it with a massive knife. Autumn was coming.

The tailor turned from his worktable and said, "Ill-gotten gain, if you believe the rumors. My neighbor saw the butcher in the park last night. He was cutting off the legs of a horse corpse with a hacksaw and then carrying the legs through the streets wrapped in a blanket. He's passing the meat off to customers as factory product, because the city has cut him off. He'd go back for the rest of the horse," said the tailor full of contempt, "if the rest weren't so complicated."

"Are you going to report him?"

"No, no. Things seem to be taking care of themselves. Anyway, it's no surprise: look at his father. Consider his son. Things like this are passed on; they advance in the line, unless the line," said the tailor, snipping his scissors at the air, "is cut." The tailor glared through the window of his shop. Ben reminded himself of his natural feelings on the matter (that the butcher, like everyone else, deserved what he got), but he felt, too, that the tailor went too far, and he said, "Times are tough."

The tailor threw his heavy, black-handled scissors into the pile of fabric on his cutting table. He pointed at Ben. "If times are tough, why am I drowning in the best-milled cotton and wool? If times are so tough, Ben, how is it possible that you are free to enjoy drinking tea and eating cookies here all day? It's possible, in a just and orderly world, that times are tough only for the unjust. I've seen other young men struggling and weakening in idiosyncratic and home-made suits, and I've seen them stumbling in the street, and it doesn't move me. They will die of the failure they have permitted to bloom in themselves as certainly as the leaves of the flowering trees will die in the first hour of winter. 'A man who will not change cannot keep his place in this world any more than a flower can resist being displaced by the fruit beneath it!'"

Ben stared at his knees; his black trousers were dusted in the powdered sugar and blond crumbs of the contents of the tailor's cookie tin. The old man was shouting the ancient words at him, killing him.

"I'm begging you to make me a suit. I'm begging you," said Ben, overcome with panic.

"What?"

"Time is running out." Ben met the tailor's look. "They're stockpiling lumber for Independence Day. The summer's winding down. I'm frightened. I'm getting very worried. You know, the feeling that time is slipping away from you, and then there will be none. I need a suit," said Ben, "I need to find a wife . . ."

"Well, what's stopping you? Do you know anything about the way the world works? Have you not heard a word I've said these last few weeks?"

"But you said . . ."

"Listen, Ben. One says many things over a lifetime, and, while most of a man's words add up to a singular lifelong complaint, and others are merely echoes of the words of one's fellows, et cetera, there is, nonetheless, a great wasteland of surprising words behind a man at my age, and so, if things I said caused you to feel hopeful, we can't be shocked by it."

"But you told me to hold out hope, to keep a positive attitude."

"Did I tell you to hold out hope? Seems unlikely," said the tailor, taking a seat in the wooden chair opposite Ben.

"I've never known anything but difficulty myself. But you're quite like everyone else, as you've pointed out to me many times, and it's no surprise that you feel entitled to happiness."

"You know my family—you knew my mother and my father."

"But it's not up to them anymore, is it? It's up to you, and you appear as you are—someone refusing life, just like your father. Life is difficult, Ben, but as you've discovered, one is required only to pass through it. Departure is assured."

The tailor, shockingly strong for such an old man, had hauled Ben from the armchair and thrown him out into the street, threatening to call the police. The butcher had stood in the window of his shop and watched.

"Young man," said the butcher in a low, warm voice (not at all what Ben expected) and opened the door to his shop: "You're welcome here." But Ben wasn't about to accept pity from the lowest of the low, and he scrambled to his feet and ran, ran until he reached the water.

In the widest part of the river, scrubby islands parted the fast-moving currents, home to derelict, rusted boats, to the former cornerstones of gun towers, part of some long-defunct system of defense; the larger islands were the haphazardly planted graveyards of failed, forgotten men like Ben. How many bachelors had been ferried across by distracted civil servants and unceremoniously dumped? What happens when the boatmen push away from the dock and row out to the men with shovels, the ones who chain-smoke and make crude jokes and roll bachelors into pits, and come back hungry, sometimes laughing themselves into coughing fits. Do anything enough—even murder—and it loses its horrible strangeness.

When he was a boy, Ben and his mother had watched the failed bachelors being marched down the street at the end of each summer, on their way to the factories, to the work crews in the park, to the river's edge, to the prison. The men in gray smocks shuffled past, and boys and girls threw apples at their feet, and rowdy men jumped down into their yards and shouted, "Throw out the trash! Throw out the trash!" until their wives cajoled them back up onto their porches, and Ben's mother rested her hands lightly on his shoulders and said, "What a shame."

A Father's Tale, Part 2

Thanks to me, the Enemy was still at large in the woods, and now I had only Buddy's pistol with which to defend myself. Every waking hour, I waited for the Enemy whom I had spared to slaughter us. I waited for him day and night. During long, silent, defensive dig-ins behind the line of pines that spring, I listened more intently than I ever had. I listened to the sounds of spring: the crackling thaw of creeks, the rush of water, the new breeze through the trees, the thrum of insects, the wingbeats and calls of the red-throated birds. I tried to listen harder, better: though these were the sounds of spring, I feared that hidden among them was the sound of the Enemy advancing, expertly cloaking his footfall in the sounds of the world.

Summer came. The ground was sun-baked hard beneath our boots, the hornets drifted peevishly between the pines. I was resting in the ovenlike shade of a tent, watching the shadows of the trees shift along the taut canvas. A trapped moth bumped against the pale interior of the tent, hitting the end, I thought, hitting the end of all he'd ever know.

A fellow soldier had tried to buck me up, admonished me to remember my wife and my son. I pictured Ben, the question-generating machinery of youth whirring endlessly in his sweet, soft head, and I thought of my wife, how she could close my eyes and hold my head against her chest, and I could hear her heart, *tump, tump,* and all was well, and, yet, *still* our little camp was a plague of mud, snakes, hornets. I no longer cared if the Enemy found us, if he hacked away at me with a dull hatchet and made a woodpile of my limbs, sliced me to ribbons under the bright seal of the noonday sun. Let him. I wouldn't raise a hand against him. He was my Enemy only because someone had forced me to grow up beside him in hatred, and now we were as close as brothers, and it was already too late. I was cursed with an Enemy in life, and he was cursed with me. We would never know peace together or away from one another.

"*Move*, soldier," seethed my commanding officer. "On your feet!" He was standing in the mouth of the tent. The wind picked up. I watched the shadow-needles of the ghostly pines rising and falling across the sun-bleached canvas overhead. I was in the bow of the ghost ship safely crossing the open sea . . . the waves were kicking at me, kicking at me.

Finally our tour of duty was up. The Enemy had never shown himself, never attacked, never so much as left a single track. We were sailing down the great river in the middle of the night, huddled together against the fresh chill in the air. "Soon you'll see your boy, Ben!" shouted a fellow soldier. The other men were jubilant, relaxed, but I was the prisoner of a lunatic thought: what if the Enemy had stowed away in my brain, where he would lie low until I was back in the heart of my life, my city, my home, my little Ben nested deep in his covers?

We had marched at full-tilt day and night to make it home in time for Independence Day, but I parted company with the other men by the old prison. "I want to visit my mother first," I said, yanking my collar and nodding grimly toward the train station and the Sheds. It was simply the first thing that came to mind—I knew I couldn't go home. I took an old postcard from my pack and wrote a quick note to my wife. I handed it to a fellow soldier whose house was near mine. "Do you mind?" I asked. "I don't want her to worry when I don't come home right away." I could hear the distant pops of hammers falling, the asthmatic hewing of the broad saws through the long planks, the shouts of men. The intolerable sounds of Independence Day.

I walked away from my bewildered brothers, out toward open country, and I thought of my mother. When one thinks of the Sheds (and, really, how many of us go out to see them for ourselves?), one thinks of the bookroom quiet, the dusky light, the "solemn hush of the countryside"—by which one means: the beautiful stoicism of women. To the very end, our mothers accompanied by birdsong and the sounds of trains and the endearing swarms of dust motes that visit them in the afternoons, when the sun cracks through the spaces between the boards and deepens the silence with light. But I preferred to think of my mother fighting for her life. I wanted her to kick at the chained doors and curse and scream and punch wildly at the boarded windows, the way young women do (or are expected to), when they refuse to marry, refuse to choose, and are entombed in the Sheds in the full bloom of youth.

I turned back toward the river and walked farther and farther out, until I had plunged back into the wilderness. I was immediately afraid. Alone in the cold woods, while my wife and son sat beside the crackling hearth and waited for the telltale sound of my boots on the front walk. I pictured Ben racing to the window and back again, at the mercy of his happy little body, a doomed little animal, all heart and appetite. But I walked deeper into the dark pinewoods, the tumultuous sea of leaves, the green-choked alleys of the creek beds. The fangs of the underbrush—it knows me, it has me, it's in me. Or my thoughts have fanged the underbrush, invented this dark green villainy. I tried to settle my mind—I knew that when I was unhappy in this way, all of life was an armory, a hall of weapons I polished with my thoughts.

Before long, the old dreaded project dangled in my brain. The villainous, mutineering hand of the mind had begun to turn its own crank. Where was this terrible volition originating (in my brain—where else)? *Where is this terrible volition originating?* A voice harangued me, followed me through the woods—I struggled to anchor it, with reason, to the center of my brain. *Where do you think you're going?* the voice sneered. The stalwart trees watched me indifferently.

"What are you doing?" I managed to ask myself aloud. But my thoughts were already re-forming the designations: the hanging vines were hangmen, the heaped leaves were pyres. I had the terrible feeling of wrongheaded lucidity that had dogged me since boyhood. I remembered suddenly that I had thrown my knife in the woods months before—I had wanted nothing more to do with it. Now, I was determined to retrace my steps to it. I knew that I was something that the universe would have to correct if it was to redeem itself in the eyes of others. I reassured myself that I was a better husband and father for limiting the liability of my wife and my son, for sparing them the elaborate negotiations in which the universe and I were now embroiled. The woods grew colder and darker, until I had to crawl on my hands and knees to feel my way.

Look at this new kind of creature crawling on the earth. The hateful voice followed me through the woods. I was listening attentively, crawling through the darkness, trying to feel my way along a steep, rocky embankment. *Saw you ALONE,* said the voice. *Thought I'd come OVER.*

I woke the next morning deep in the woods—I was hopelessly lost, exhausted. I stared overhead, through the layers and layers of indifferent and alien leaves, beyond which the sky was pale and bright. I thought of the sameness of the leaves in the city, how abundant but ordinary leaves represent a profusion of Life, but perhaps one not worth living. I was a mere man, but I could add to the beauty of the world. I slid down the embankment to the river's edge. The soft green shapes of the algae-carpeted rocks were above the waterline and drying in the sun; the pink and gray granites, house-sized boulders of rock veined with quartz, looked in the autumnal light like tombs of silver and gold. I stood at the water's edge and looked to the opposite shore. Wheresoever the Enemy goes, we must follow.

SEPTEMBER

Dread, dread September if you are alone, Young Man.
Hide among the rotting timbers, separate, separated:
All are lost and none remembered
In the slaughter yard of old Dreadtember.
Dead timber, remember, septic soil and no end
To Dreadtember, when the taut rope and creak of timber
Will teach you again to dread September.

Ben

The front door to the Bachelor House had swelled in the heat and was stuck open at an angle that permitted flies, hornets, mice, rats, dogs, and cockroaches to come and go freely but required a man of average size (Ben) to scrape between the door and the frame. He squeezed through, tearing another hole in his jacket, and climbed the stairs, listening to his own heavy footfall stamp the soft, ominous silence with a sad tempo. The halls were silent; he counted the closed doors . . . four, five, six . . . and pictured doomed bachelors behind each one, catatonic men in bed, staring, starving, waiting for the liberating "My brother!" of the Brothers of Mercy swarming the house. Up and down the street, the Bachelor Houses were dying their annual deaths. The rooms were cold and dark as empty cupboards, there was the smell of old kitchen grease congealing, there were the muddy tracks and leaf scrub drying out in the front hall. At night, the house creaked like an abandoned ship phantoming through the swells.

The door to Selfridge's room had stood open for days: another lucky man hurrying toward the warmth of an embrace that—what could possibly harm or alter a human being who loved and was loved?

In Selfridge's room still lived the many guns, another bachelor skill happily abandoned by its practitioner. There were guns lined neatly on the shelves and others depicted in posters hanging on the wall. Rows and rows: guns with flintlocks, those with hammerlocks, those known to misfire, those to be used in a duel, those carved of cherrywood, those with etched mother-of-pearl handles, those with the names of women, those with the names of generals, and those that were black and plain—the ones that seemed to be everywhere. Ben took one off the shelf and picked up a few bullets, which were scattered across the floor. Selfridge had shot out his window, leaving only the bullet-nicked white frame and the picture of the world.

Ben sat on the windowsill and loaded the gun. He aimed at the tree in the yard and fired, sending the birds into the air and the squirrels winding frantically down the tree. There was no denying the pleasure: he had made that happen. He made things happen! He fired again and watched the animals draining from the branches. At the base of the tree, they scattered along the ground, while the birds, able by virtue of flight to keep the problem in play, lifted, alighted, lifted, alighted.

Then Ben heard shouts in the house, someone struggling with the front door. He shoved the gun into his pocket and ran out into the hall. Finton was on the landing, peering down the stairs.

"Oh, my God," said Ben. "They're here, they're here."

"Who's here?"

"The Brothers of Mercy are coming. No, no, no . . ."

"I don't think so—not yet. Calm down, Ben."

"Finton, please," whispered Ben in a near panic. Did Finton not grasp that they had finally come for him? For his lack of concern in matters of this world, for their very serious consequences. For his noted absence from the world. For his long occupation of a place (a Bachelor House—worse, his mother's house!) designed for a discreet experience, a tightly contained form of youth (exuberance alternating with melancholy) from which one must move on. "Just go back to your room, Finton. And close the door."

"Ben, I can help—I've been through all this before."

"Finton! I don't think you understand your situation. It's not a normal situation. Please just hide."

Ben could hear some new and brutal force pushing at the door. He considered jumping from one of the second-story windows but pushed past Finton instead so he could peer down the stairs at the door. He could see someone trying to squeeze into the house—it was only a policeman! "I'll handle this," said Ben. He jogged down the stairs, buttoning his jacket as he went. He poked his head amiably through the opening in the door.

"Officers."

Two policemen stood on the front steps. Several others milled through the yard, studying the grass, inspecting the flower beds. Ben smiled and buttoned the top button of his dark coat. Perhaps Selfridge is a wanted man, Ben thought hopefully.

The policemen stared.

"Sir," said the shorter officer.

"Officers," said Ben again, disliking the thin timbre of his voice. "Has something happened to Selfridge?"

The other officer, inexpressive and tall, wrote in his notebook: *Selfridge?*

"Who is Selfridge?"

"One of us, a former boarder bachelor—I mean bachelor boarder. He's married, or, I should say, he is *getting* married."

The policemen smiled at one another fondly and took a step forward. The tall one said, "And you're jealous? Had your eye on his girl maybe?"

"No, of course not."

"Come out here, why don't you?"

Ben pushed his way through and stood on the front step with the officers.

"And who are you?" asked the short one, giving Ben an official look: gentle, predatory.

"Beh," said Ben nervously.

"Ben," corrected the tall officer.

The short officer gave a friendly smile: "Seems you've been treading on the tailor's good nature."

"What?"

"Even the tailor's generosity has its limits. He has notified us of his intention to stop carrying you."

"What?"

"You must vacate this house immediately. Unless you want to be charged with illegal occupation of a house."

"Wait. I paid him—"

The short officer regarded the tall one in disbelief. "Please tell me he isn't going to argue with us."

"Wait. Please listen," said Ben.

"Get your things—five minutes," interrupted the tall one and rested his hand casually on his pistol.

Ben thought of his paintings and bounded back up the stairs. He crammed the military cap, cufflinks, and paint pigments into his satchel. He took Selfridge's gun from his pocket and tucked it into his satchel beneath his father's cap. He yanked the canvases from the wall and scanned the room. He had nothing else. "Finton?" Finton's door stood open; he was nowhere in sight. Ben could hear the policemen climbing the stairs.

"I'm leaving, I'm leaving now!" Ben shouted. The two officers were inspecting the upstairs hall, glancing casually into open rooms.

"Well, go on, then," said the shorter officer and smiled.

"Thank you," said Ben, wanting, perversely, to please the friendly man who was ruining his life.

He walked to the park, clutching his satchel. Maybe he could patch things up with the tailor somehow, or perhaps Albert would let him stay for a few days? Ben circumvented the bachelors' hill, the late-summer crush of bachelors jockeying for space, looking for women, all of whom seemed to be avoiding the park. In the near distance, Ben could see workers making repairs to the Independence Day stage. His brain was laying down the law: no more stupid daydreams, no more cowardice, no more wasting time. Bachelors elbowed and shoved one another; they fell down in the damp grass and swung wildly at one another. Policemen looked on, tired and bored. Ben could feel his hands seizing into fists, his heart swelling with hatred at the sight of the police. He glared at the facade of the station, making no effort to conceal his contempt for it. The doors to the police station swung open; two policemen emerged carrying an unconscious man half-covered by a blanket. Ben smiled awkwardly at the policemen, his hatred converting immediately into a look of friendly submission. The police made small talk while they carried the man toward the river. They were followed in a few seconds by another pair of policemen, carrying another body down the station steps. Bachelors were dropping like flies.

Ben walked to the back of the station to take refuge in the overgrown alley. He hid in the gray-green light, trying to think of what to do next. If he went back to the house, perhaps Finton would hide him there—he would know every secret of the old house, having grown up there.

As his eyes adjusted to the low light, he made out the shape of a man lying on the ground: He was wearing a pale suit; one leg was bent awkwardly beneath the other. A blanket covered the man's face. Ben fell to his knees and lifted the corner of the blanket: no one he knew.

The bachelor's mouth hung open slightly. "Brother?" Ben said flatly and nudged him. Nothing. Ben took the man's hand in his hand and held it for a long moment. He leaned in and said, "It's OK, Brother. Everything will be all right."

Ben took off his dark coat and laid it on the grass. He removed the pale jacket of the bachelor, rolling him this way and that; he dusted off the back of the pale jacket; he put it on; he buttoned the buttons. Ben exchanged his pants with those of the bachelor, who was suddenly coming to, trying to speak, reaching weakly for Ben with his hands. Ben was wearing the pale pants and trying to get the black pants past the other man's knees. "Shhhh," soothed Ben. "It's all right. I'm sorry, Brother." Ben turned his back to the man's face so that he could straddle his chest and pull the black trousers into place; he buttoned them quickly. The man was forming words, as of yet unintelligible. These would be the accusations, thought Ben dispassionately, the pleas for mercy. "You'll be OK, Brother, if you'll just keep still," he said over his shoulder.

Ben crouched behind the bachelor and propped him

up, so that he could thread his arms through the sleeves of the stinking old black jacket. "Listen closely: the tailor did this to you," Ben whispered and then let the bachelor fall back onto the ground. "Here," he said, pressing his satchel into the man's hand. "I'm giving you all that I have in the world."

Ben checked the pockets of the pale jacket—a train ticket and an invitation to the last Listening Party of the season. "You're in no shape to attend a Listening Party," said Ben, unable to conceal his delight. The bachelor opened his eyes and stared. Ben pressed his hand over the man's eyes until he felt them close again. He touched the man's face gently; he smoothed the hair away from the man's feverish forehead, comforting him. "Quiet now. Go back to sleep, Brother."

Ben walked toward the bachelors' hill, buttoning and unbuttoning his new jacket with pleasure. He could feel his mind settling into the simple hierarchy it had been designed for: he was happy, despite everything. He unbuttoned the jacket again to inspect the lining more closely: orchid-pale silk ghosted with a lavender pattern—bees? Bees, decided Ben, faintly, faintly living within the silk. *Lo, when I wore the pale suit I did proceed . . .*

He plunged into the rough crowd on the hill, the grass worn, rutted, and muddy. He shoved his way happily ahead. Other bachelors careened into him and slapped his back with painful and powerful camaraderie. Ben felt the tight bubble of feeling that filled his chest for so long burst, and he pushed his way energetically past other men, knocking them almost from their feet. The sun was at the top of the sky, and it was still summer, and the birds were telling high-pitched, mellifluous secrets to one another, and the flowers were flush and full and bending their stems, and he was in the city he loved, in the heart of the park he loved. Anything was possible!

Once beyond the bachelors' hill, Ben made his way to the train station. He tried to effect a purposeful, jaunty walk—another lucky bachelor making a routine departure for the countryside. He felt he could extend endlessly this new project of being a normal, happy man. But when he thought of Finton, his heart plunged. *Don't think about it,* chided his brain. *How can I not?* he hissed back, thinking of the green velvet chair in Finton's room, which he had grown to love—the flecks of tobacco, the spilled tea, the dark lines where Finton's hands had rested habitually on the outer seam.

Meeks

It wasn't unusual, toward the end of summer, to find civil servants, like dying hornets, whole but done for, lying in the grass at night. I was passing through the alley behind the police station, on my way back to the Captain, when I came across a young man sleeping in the grass. It is not a policeman's job to pass judgment, of course, merely to maintain the order of things and to describe what he sees in an orderly fashion. It struck me right away that there was something both comical and dire about the man's situation. Dire in that he was alone in an alley in the middle of the night, and comical in that he was wearing a funny little suit—*despite* the direness. Or perhaps he had fallen asleep a boy and grown overnight into a man. His jacket reached only to his belly button, but his shirt was of a very fine fabric that glowed in the sepulchral light of the alley.

I poked the man's hand gently with a stick, and then the side of his face, which was soft and young and handsome. I poked it again with the stick and said, Brother?

Nothing.

A satchel lay near the man's head; I searched it. (I'm a policeman.) Odds and ends, mostly. Some squares of canvas, which might have made excellent boot liners had they not been ruined for the purpose by layers of paint. And then, at the bottom of the satchel, I found a gun. I had never held a gun in my life. I lifted it reverently, fearfully out of the satchel, and I saw the gleam of its black fang in the moonlight.

I leaned against the hard wall of the police station and considered my options. I held the gun, which was cold and heavy and beautiful to the touch, and contemplated the young man. Bodies in the park are invariably a nuisance, attracting dogs and thieves and sick adventurers in the dark hours before the garbagemen carry them away. But I considered that this body was both a problem of the generic type and of a rare type (e.g., *an opportunity*). The dying and the dead can sometimes be found lying quietly by the docks, or in other dark places, not quite underfoot but among us, just beyond the scope of our errands, and there they wait patiently until we come to collect. Perhaps this young man was here for me, cosmically speaking. And in exchange for the misdemeanor of circumventing Bedge's forms, I resolved to deliver this body to him—an innocent victim, a wanted man? In either case, Bedge would have a stake in things.

Even a shallow grave proves challenging if one is not properly equipped. I hid the gun in the ripped lining of my coat, and I broke a slat from a discarded park chair and began to stab away at the earth, scraping back the grass and cutting through the net of roots that held the soil in place. I dug and dug, stopping every now and then to toss aside the rocks I unearthed or to roll into the hole I was digging in order to judge its depth.

When I was satisfied, or at least too tired to go on, I took hold of the man's ankles and dragged him down the alley. It was difficult work. I had to stop once or twice to rest, but eventually, I got the body into the hole; arranged his legs carefully, so that his feet fell into place; and saw that it was a very tight fit, much too narrow for this surprisingly strong young man. Something about our relative positions in this little drama had led me to underestimate the breadth of his shoulders, and I had to stand on one of his shoulders with all my weight in order to force the body down into the grave, and then the man convulsed, and there was terrified screaming (his and mine), and a hand shot up and coiled around my ankle, and I saw that the terrible white eyes were staring up at me, and I tore myself away, falling to the ground, and then scrambled blindly away, until I dared look over my shoulder. I watched the man struggle to roll out of the little grave or to sit up. I felt that my hand was burning with pain—I had sliced it open on the broken slat when I fell.

The young man seemed truly stuck, and once I sensed that he was giving up again, I crawled back to his side and whispered into his ear, You'll be OK, Brother. I'll take care of you, little brother, watch over you until morning, and the young man held his hand feebly over his face as if in terror. I removed his boots and one of his socks, which I bound around my injured hand—My apologies, I said. I seem to be bleeding quite profusely.

I lay beside him all night, talking at length, sometimes

touching his face reassuringly, as my mother often did when I was afraid in the park at night, and we lay there together, and to reassure him, I told him to imagine that we were boys, brothers hiding together in the park, waiting, listening for Mother, and when she called out, that would be the end of the game of hiding, and he would go home, and everything would be all right. He stared into the night sky and listened, he sometimes said *God, no, no, no,* presumably in answer to some internal question, he wept, he sweated profusely, he made strange oaths to the heavens, raising more than once the specter of his own mother, etc. He struggled once or twice to wrench himself from the hole, and then finally he slept, just as the dawn came, and the trees turned silver in the gray-green light.

I lay beside my brother, and I listened to the garbagemen making their way through the park. When they reached us, they formed their ominous circle around me, but I was happy and at ease, and I leaned back casually on my elbow and said, Brothers? And, for once, they did not dally but walked away quickly and were gone. I studied the face of the young man beside me—he looked very peaceful.

After a few minutes, I heard the unmistakable sound of policemen running from the station, an occasional crack as they ran heedlessly through the low, dry branches of the trees. Here! I shouted, so that Bedge would know where to find me, and I could see the shapes of men jumping between the trees, and I could hear them shouting breathlessly into their two-way radios as they got close.

Bedge told me to wait outside the police station. He and the rookies carried the man into the station, and the door slammed shut behind them. I paced back and forth in front of the big windows, so that Bedge could see me and be reminded of who had been so instrumental in the delivery of the body to the rightful authorities. I studied the sky with scientific interest, as if I were testing a system of predictions about which I had thus far only theorized in a scientific notebook. I was enjoying myself. I was happy the universe had given me my gun, and I was glad I had brought comfort to one of my brothers when he was hurt and afraid.

I waited and waited, until the sun hung low over the river and the oyster sky was reflected in the big, gray windows of the police station. The station was eerily quiet; the door was shut, sealed like a tomb, and I could see nothing in the windows except for the reflection of early-evening light. I could hear the *tock, tock, tock* of hooves on distant streets. Finally, I couldn't stand it any longer, and I climbed the old stone steps, and I pulled open the door, and I entered the station stealthily as a penitent in felt-soled shoes. I saw that Bedge and the other officers were huddled around a table. Bedge turned and saw me and nudged a rookie, who pulled me to the other side of the station before I could see what was on the table.

The rookie and I went to a quiet corner, and he leaned in close to my face.

Please, have a seat, he said. We'll have to file an official report.

I would like to talk to Bedge, I said.

You mean, the Chief of Police?

Yes.

Did he attack you first?

Who, Bedge?

The rookie gave me a long quiet look, and once he had taken the full measure of some esoteric quantity he seemed to think I possessed, he said, No, the victim.

The victim? I looked at Bedge's back, wanted to call out to him.

The victim is a bachelor, protected under the law.

Oh, right. The victim. Yes, I protected him all night.

I see. Do you have negative feelings toward bachelors? I know I sometimes do, he said kindly and smiled.

I like them, I said.

And the police?

Well, I am a policeman, I said. Therefore: et cetera, et cetera.

And the man in the black jacket?

The man in the black jacket?

Yes. I'm just wondering if you might've mistaken this young man whom you found in a black jacket—or, in order to fulfill a fantasy, perhaps placed in a black jacket—for the man in the black jacket?

The man in the black jacket?

The rookie sighed a deep policeman's sigh and continued, It's just my observation that the serious nature of the man's wounds, even setting aside for a moment his death, suggests a wild attack, something animal and personal. Did you kill the young man believing in the heat of the moment that you had encountered your nemesis?

No, no, no. We were playing a game, and then he slept.

What kind of a game?

That we were brothers, I said, my face hot with childish shame.

So you struck him with pleasure, as if playing a game, and then he seemed to fall asleep.

He wouldn't fit into the little grave, I said earnestly.

Hmmm . . . but is that the kind of game you would play with a brother, pretending to bury him?

He was dead, and then he was alive, and only then did

we play a game—we were hiding together in the park.

Aha, said the young officer. I think I understand now. Jealousy between brothers is an old and difficult game— possibly the oldest. Don't be too hard on yourself.

Thank you, I said, now can I please speak to Bedge? He knows that I am my mother's only son and a dedicated policeman. I would never harm anyone, except perhaps one, I said, laughing politely at the extension of our little joke.

The rookie raised his eyebrows: And who in particular would that be?

The man in the black jacket, I said a little incredulously. You're the one who brought him up!

The rookie was studying my hand with concern. What happened here? he asked.

There was a misunderstanding, I said vaguely. I cut my hand. Then my brother gave me his sock since I was bleeding.

Why don't you go over to the freezer there and get some ice for your hand. That looks like a nasty cut.

Thank you, I said, relaxing again into the familiar atmosphere of the old station.

I opened the station icebox and stared into the ice fog swarming the bottled drinks and cherry pops. I'd already forgotten what I was doing there—I was worried about the gun. What Bedge would do if he discovered that I had shown criminally wild disregard for the forms he loved. *Ah, but there's the Chief of the Police, and then there's the Universe . . .*

Meeks!

I jumped. Bedge was waving me over to the table. I was happy that my face was numb with cold so it could betray none of my feelings. Several rookies were still crowded around the table, on which were laid, with forensic neatness, the satchel, a military cap (We can't trace this, said Bedge, it's a fake), and six squares of canvas, painted on both sides.

Bedge said, A great deal about an individual's criminality can be discerned through a study of his things. What do you make of these canvases, Meeks?

They look ruined, I said.

I can't even tell what some of these things are, said a rookie.

Paintings, I said.

No shit. I can't tell what they're *of*.

I believe those are lemons, said another rookie, pointing to a cluster of yellow circles.

Or oranges?

Maybe these things aren't his, I said, remembering the antifanciful way in which the victim had played (or not played) our game. Maybe they belong to the man who attacked him.

Bedge shook his head. Meeks, they're telling me that you attacked him.

I didn't!

I believe you, but there has to be an investigation, an *internal* investigation. Once everything is cleared up, you can return to being a police officer, of course. I'll need your hat.

It won't come off.

Meeks, no more games.

I bowed, offering any of the rookies the opportunity to wrestle with my head.

Ben

Ben boarded the last northbound train with innocent calm, strolled into the first car, and yawned, his mind a nest of panic and disproportion. He took his seat, surveyed the car: it seemed to be populated exclusively by old women. He was surrounded by old women. Too late to move. He was in the women's car, disaster. Women in cloth coats with fur collars. These were *old* women. The wind cut in through a faulty window and ruffled the fur collar of an elderly lady, who smiled at him. He smiled back drowsily and smoothed the lapels of his new suit and was immediately comforted by it, by the renewed, even extreme, degree of his relative youth. Ben had smiled, but he reconsidered; these are the very people rolling steadily away from the center of life, out toward the Sheds. *Why am I with them?*

"Where's this train headed?" he asked the old woman beside him.

"Oh, *please*," she said, her tone incredulous and hurt and stern (motherly). She turned to gaze out the window. Ben pulled the paper ticket from his breast pocket. Rows of numbers and letters. . . . He became unaccountably afraid. He glanced at the old woman, wished she would say something soothing. He wanted her to tell him the story of where they were going and what would happen when they got there. The conductor entered the car, punched the tickets. Two young men among so many old women. Ben felt he could ask him anything. He had learned that anything could be a pretense for conversation, especially between men. "Friend, when do you think we'll get in?"

"Get in where?" The conductor tipped his plastic-lined hat back from his forehead; he clicked together the metal teeth of the ticket-puncher impatiently. Ben looked to the conductor and to the old woman for guidance, and they gazed back, as if upon the face of their own weak and unpromising son.

"Your ticket!"

Ben handed it over unsteadily. The conductor punched it. He moved on, punching the tickets of the old women.

"I'm on my way to a Listening Party," said Ben, looking out at the blurred, green-gray world that ringed the city center. He twisted the buttons on his jacket.

"How wonderful for you," said the old woman. "I met my husband at a Listening Party. He is now deceased."

"My parents met at a Listening Party."

"And are *they* deceased?"

"They are."

"Thought so. Things tend to head that way. But I wish you the best of luck."

The world slid by as the train sped up, past the muddy suck of the river's widening edge, the buckling balconies and shallow back porches, the haggard light posts and chipped hollow wooden stairs, the blunt, blind fire hydrants, the barrel-vaulted worlds beneath the footbridges, worlds of sooty paint and swallows' nests.

The train passed the oldest Sheds, fields of green huts beside the tracks. Hefty chains were snaked through the metal door handles and padlocked. That seems excessive, thought Ben, who had never actually visited the Sheds. On each shed was stenciled a name . . . *Lucia, Nancy, Henrietta* . . . the names flew by. The old woman covered her face with her hands; tense silence overtook the car. Ben's heart seized him—he thought of his mother, consigned to a life of *serene contemplation* in one of the named but numberless rooms. He imagined peering through the Shed doors and seeing his mother upright at a little writing desk, thinking or reading

. . . or what? Why hadn't he found her Shed his first day back and torn the chain from the handle and carried her out into the sunlight and cared for her for the rest of her life? (Because it was forbidden.) The train slowed. The old woman leaned close and whispered to Ben, "I believe this is you."

He seemed to be the only one at the weathered little station. He surveyed the countryside with the sentimental eye of an urban dweller faced at last with the real rolling hills, with the smoke from anonymous and modest chimneys in the distance—all precisely as it should be.

He followed the only road leading from the train station and saw no one and heard no one until dusk, when he passed a middle-aged woman sweeping the porch of her farmhouse. She pointed farther down the road before Ben could shout a greeting. His heart expanded—he was a young man in a pale suit on his way to a Listening Party, and even the flint-eyed wariness of these suburbanites was a pleasure, a pleasure precisely to the degree that it confirmed, for better or worse, the fact of what he had become. It was evening, and the countryside was falling into an eerie rural quiet, and he turned up the collar of his fine pale jacket against the chill.

At last, Ben saw the warm yellow windows of a country estate at the end of a gravel path, holy-seeming beneath an archway of white poplar branches. He took the path reverently, listened to his boots crunching through the gravel. He went to an open door at the side of the house and found a dozen men and women seated around a wooden table, eating dinner in a desultory and determined way. The woman nearest the door started when she saw him.

"Are you lost?"

"I hope not," said Ben and grinned pleasantly.

The diners put down their forks at once and stared.

"Everyone's out," said the woman.

"Out?"

"Out for the night."

"Well, I'll turn in early then," said Ben agreeably—he was a man on top of his own affairs but not *pompously* so. The group stared at him dimly. He tried to speak more clearly. "Where. Should. I. Sleep?"

"I'm sorry. There's been some mistake," she said, leaning forward into the candlelight and speaking to Ben as if he were a child. "All rooms are taken. But there's a little room upstairs, which you can use tonight, and we'll sort things out in the morning."

"A little room will be just fine, thank you."

Again, stillness overtook the diners.

"And the little room," said Ben, "is . . . ?"

One of the men stood abruptly, knocking his chair back. "Fine. Your *luggage*?"

"I have none," said Ben.

The women gave him an appraising look. He ignored it. His heart felt light—he was free of guilt. If the universe was not constructed (as it clearly was not) so that his happiness was a product of the same natural order that forged foals, flowers, thunderstorms, then he must fight with everything he had to make it his.

Meeks

I sat at the feet of Captain Meeks and watched the phantom masses preparing for Independence Day—perfect strangers sharing the air in deep, satisfying breaths, the people filling up with affection for the past. Every few minutes, I would peer into my coat to see that the gun was still there, shining like a deadly viper I had trained to sleep in peace against my heart.

I detected the smell of old sugar being burned off the industrial mixers. I tuned my ear to the sounds of construction, invisible within the fog. The hammering seemed to be coming from overhead, as if the workmen were hammering on the pale hardtops of low-lying clouds. Married men were showing off their autumn sweaters, light and clean, newly unfolded from beds of tissue paper. In every household, a man kneels beside the old cedar-lined chest and gazes upon his autumn sweater: a reunion! The excitement of the new season, the pleasure of this gentle reinvention. When people burst unexpectedly into the little clearing where I was sitting, every detail of their faces painfully sharp in the dilute white light of the afternoon, and seeing me materialize, as it were, out of the fog, they faltered in speech and stride, tightened their grips on their objects unconsciously, and continued down the fog-locked park path. Look at those cake boxes! Those fine, folded corners, that comical striped string. I watched as neighbors overcame the wariness that kept them quiet the rest of the year and shouted out to one another in the park—Hey there! and How *are* you? Impending festivities make city dwellers reckless.

Mother and I used to spend hours together watching this procession, listening for the construction of the Independence Day platform, admiring the parade of autumn sweaters. The man in the black jacket sometimes idled nearby in a stand of tall, thin trees, until my mother went to him, and I pretended not to mind. I decided this unspoken agreement between my mother and the man in the black jacket was a special form of adult nonchalance, which, however conspicuous, should be respectfully allowed to remain unacknowledged or at least unaltered by me—a mere boy—who might have changed it by speaking. Or, I sensed that my mother required my silence, and so I was silent.

Ben

In the room above the kitchen, Ben found a narrow bed, a wooden chair missing several slats, a man's sock, and a collection of empty bottles under a tiny porcelain sink in the corner. The room was possibly smaller than his room at the Bachelor House.

He undressed, arranging his suit carefully on the broken chair, and rinsed his underwear and socks with ice-cold water in the sink. He draped them over the radiator and crawled into the sour-smelling bed. He watched his long black socks drip water onto the filthy floor.

There was no top sheet on the bed. The coarse blanket irritated his skin, and he was often startled awake by the sensation of the rough blanket having coiled itself around his ankles while he shivered, naked and cold in the open air. He hadn't been able to find the light switch and folded the rancid pillow over his face to block out the dull, persistent light of the overhead bulb. He tried to lie very still; he stared into the foul blackness of the pillow. The narrow bed shook over the hulking machines in the kitchen. In the middle of the night, he flipped through some old society magazines that lay on the floor beside the bed. Bachelor House 902 was not listed. So what? There were other lists, better lists.

Just as he drifted into sleep, dogs started yelping at the early morning fog. The house staff ground coffee, chattered, crunched across the gravel courtyard noisily. Then he was oppressed by the stage whispers of people outside his door. "Is he awake? Should we wake him? Are you awake in there?"

"In a minute!" Ben shouted as cheerfully as he could, and the voices disappeared.

Ben dressed, pulling on warm, dry underwear, warm, dry socks. His shirt, admittedly, stank—he would wash it tonight in the sink; he tucked the shirt into the perfect, flat-front pale trousers. He spat on his boots and polished them with the dirty sock in the corner. He plunged his arms gleefully into the cool, silk corridors of the jacket sleeves. He shrugged the shoulders into place and buttoned the jacket, feeling hung with a mantle of impervious white mist.

He stepped out into the hall; he could hear the buzz of voices downstairs; he hesitated. One or two bachelor voices boomed above the others, and then the sound of a laughing crowd. But there was no way to move except forward. He forced himself to descend the stairs and walk into the main room, already packed with young women and bachelors in pale suits. Ben eyed the young women as they passed: poised and animated; attentive and preoccupied; loud and shy; boyishly thin and soft, plump.

Someone handed Ben a drink. He finished it quickly and went in pursuit of another. He leaned against the wall and drank, keeping his eye out for young women left unattended. But they were never unattended. The bachelors were relentless, double- and triple-teaming women, boring them to death; and he decided to bide his time, to cultivate an air of mystery: the thinking man's strategy.

When the bachelors headed out to the fields to shoot, Ben hung back. He wandered the house, investigating its strange objects, the solemn faces on the walls, portraits of the presumably dead sitting in moody lightning-cracked landscapes or under the boughs of fruit-laden trees.

It had started to rain. Ben wandered downstairs into the kitchen. A young man, one of the cooks, was working by the gray light of an enormous window. Steam choked the bottom two rows of windowpanes, and a thin sheet of water sluiced over the edge of the roof into the muddy, gutted side yard. A heap of slender, black branches was on the counter-top beside twin metal bowls of fruit. The cook worked down the branches with a paring knife, stripping off the clustered yellow and pink flowers, tossing them aside.

"Should I turn on the light?"

The young man looked up and raised his eyebrows expectantly. "Sir?"

"Must be hard to see what you're doing."

"The electricity is out in this part of the house. I'm used to it."

"Electricity," said Ben, rolling his eyes comically. He baffled himself. The cook ignored him. Ben could smell the cut flowers. The water rushing over the roof gave him the feeling of being behind a waterfall. It struck him that he would like to live so simply—to stay right here with the cook and learn to handle the things of this world with such easy confidence. "Can I help?" asked Ben.

The cook hesitated and scanned the kitchen uncomfortably. "Are you sure, sir? The other bachelors are out hunting."

"Please—I'd like to. I'm Ben, by the way."

"Well . . . Ben, we do need a few more oranges, lemons, and limes—the trees are behind the house about a hundred feet." He handed Ben a canvas sack and an enormous carving knife. Ben stared at them unhappily. "Sure. My pleasure."

Ben marched through the rain clutching the canvas sack and the knife—he had only wanted to stay in the warm, dim kitchen with the young man. He supposed he had brought this on himself.

Ben reached the stand of fruit trees, dark-limbed and green with wet leaves. Yellow, red, orange, and pale-green orbs shone among the branches, behind the veil of rain. It was beautiful and strange, like something Finton would have painted. He glanced back at the house and saw the silhouette of the cook standing with someone else in the window and watching him, possibly laughing.

Ben took a slender branch in his hand and bent it low. So he had been sent on a fool's errand by his new friend the cook. Fine. Drops of rain hit the small and deep green leaves, making them dip and spring. What had the cook ever accomplished? Ben's great-great-great-grandfathers had subjugated the wilderness and settled this land, and the cook had the nerve to send him out into the mud to nick fruit trees with a kitchen knife? Ben was descended from people who had taken all that they needed from life: leveled forests, gouged mountains, harnessed rivers, tamed this world so the cook could tousle it with a soft wooden spoon. They had taken their revenge in blood, and they had *invented* the long-form conversation that was the lifeblood of the old tales—and *Ben* was being made to feel the fool?

A bucket, overturned and half-sunk in the mud, pinged quietly under the rain. Several of the trees had been slashed for sap, which was collected and trucked to the city. Ben studied the slashed trees; they made him unaccountably sad. The rain picked up, pouring over the sagging brim of his hat; his suit had darkened in the downpour to a deep cream color. The oranges shone, plump and bright in the light gray rain: He was as useless as a boy in a hatchery of suns. He wanted to lie down, to stretch out beneath the trees, to be absorbed by the wet green ground; his suit, already soaked, would be ruined. The small and dark green leaves shook, hit by rainfall; the smell of soil was everywhere: it was so dark and damp with life, he wanted to lie down in it.

"Ben? Ben!"

Ben stepped back and tried to peer through the veil of rainy trees.

"Ben!" She was calling his name, she was walking right at him. He was afraid to be holding the knife and dropped it.

"Ben," she said, when she was closer, "come inside, please. It's raining."

A Brother's Tale, Part 3

Last night I dreamed that the Brothers of Mercy had me pinned to the ground. They were hunched over me, their heads silhouetted by the setting sun. They were swabbing my face with a strong-smelling cloth that made me want to fight, and I struggled and fought with all my strength, which seemed to amount to nothing. They cut away my pale suit, and then they brought over the park bum and forced him to lick my naked body. I was disgusted—by the smell of him, by the feel of his coarse, wet tongue on my skin, by his muffled voice crying out in protest and revulsion as the Brothers of Mercy pushed his head down again and again. It was almost more than I could bear, but the dream took mercy on me and dropped me in the bow of an old whaler, painted blue and black and white, sailing upriver toward the Mountain Lakes, where our parents had taken us as boys, where the hearth was always hot and the world silent and white, the sleeping bees and foxes waiting in the dark for the golden fuzz and mint green of spring. When I was a boy and I used my brain for other things! Some men were carving up a whale on the shore: clouds of fat fell open in the sun. Some men are innocent, I thought, and others are not, but all seemed well with the world again. The clear, cold water split around the bow. Then I heard a soft thumping, the *thunk . . . thunk* that always invaded my dreams, and I looked over my shoulder and saw that my brother was in the boat with me. He was slumped beside the fishing lantern; the lantern cast a thin gold light over the water as it swung back and forth, cutting into my brother's head.

I woke up, sighed with relief when I saw that we were still safely in our little room by the train station. There was my brother, passed out on his bed of coats. I liked to watch over him, just as our mother watched over us when we were boys, leaning over our soft round heads in the dark, dreaming about what we might become. Poor Mother. All of our relationships deform us (i.e., make us "human"), but how do these loving creatures (our mothers) survive the person-imploding disappointments of their sons?

By the time I turned sixteen, I knew who and what I was (an artist). I told my mother that I planned not to marry, but rather to live and die in the theater. After the briefest hesitation, she gave me a wry smile. She was masking internal panic with an amused look—oldest tactic in the book. Then she began to recite the Old Prisoner's Tale, the grisly tale of "impossible choices" that she had told us almost every night when we were boys. "Do you know the story about the old prisoner?" she said. I had no choice but to listen, and I sat at the kitchen table with her and buried my face in my hands and mumbled, "Yes, but it feels good to remember."

"They told the Old Prisoner that they would set him free—on *one* condition. He must saw off his own hands—*both* of them. They gave him a handsaw. There was nothing else in his cell—not so much as a dead *spider*. Well, he saw what kind of choice he'd been given—it was an *impossible* choice. And so, with dignity, he chose to live out his years in prison. It was a life with some limits, but it was *life.*"

"That's your interpretation," I said. "I think he just chose to live in his own head, where there are no limits—to go insane rather than accept that his life had been predicated on a lie."

"I don't understand you at all."

That night, I watched my brother helping my mother in the kitchen. They were mocking me, asking if the Great Artist would prefer carrots or squash for dinner. I decided that these cheap amusements were a kind of foreign import loaded onto local heads (my mother's, my brother's) and that they would come around in time. They didn't.

Then they had left me no choice but to fail into my art. I calculated the exact grade of failure necessary, so that I could slide, failing, into what I really wanted: the life of an artist. But the life of an artist is an impecunious one, and I was forced to dine often at my mother's house, collapsing my sense of outrage into a dense, hot, bright star that I hid in my heart while I filled my belly and fantasized about the day when I would come home a star of the theater, beloved by the people, worshipped by my mother. It was the kind of game I'd always loved to play: the entertainment of false alternatives.

Now I was a grown man, of course, making my own decisions. If my life was once a project for which another (namely, my mother) had the highest hopes, then I was *choosing* now to build a pyre under it, to use as firewood the life my mother had made and cared for.

I'd been sneaking gunpowder from the workshed behind the police station for weeks, hiding it in the upturned cuff of my work pants, which could be easily explained away—I was a clumsy workman, presumably weak with hunger and disease, shakily sorting the gunpowder.

My brother came home from his shift at the gum factory and set down three murky bottles of bad spirits, which the factory workers brewed illegally in the storerooms.

"What are you doing?" he asked.

"What are *you* doing?" I said. "That stuff will kill you."

"You're one to talk."

"I don't go near gum liquor," I said, touching the scar on my forehead delicately.

"Is that gunpowder?"

"Why, yes it is, Brother. I've been bringing a little home every day," I said, and poured the gunpowder through a makeshift paper funnel into one of our empty tea envelopes. I filed the envelope in the wooden tea box. "See? I've thought of everything."

"I don't understand what you're doing."

"I'm making a bomb," I whispered, and I was deeply gratified by the look of surprise and fear on my brother's face.

"You're trying to make a bomb?"

"No, Brother. I *am* making one."

"And what are you going to do with this bomb?"

"I'm going to destroy the city and everyone in it."

"On Independence Day?"

"That's right. On Independence Day."

"How much gunpowder is there?"

"Almost a whole tea box."

My brother picked up one of the tea envelopes I had filled with gunpowder. "There's enough in this box to blow your head off, or mine, maybe crack the Reynolds Branch. That's it. Then the play will go on . . ." While some part of me conceded that he was probably right—he had always been the more practical brother—I pretended not to understand.

Just last week, I was dropping a pinch of gunpowder into my upturned cuff when a Brother of Mercy burst into the room. I let out a small scream. He was out of breath, full of predatory intensity. He took a long, hard look at me and said, "Did you see him?"

I hesitated, wanting to understand the rules of our game better before I jumped in. "Did you see something?" he said.

"I'm sorry, see?"

"See the prisoner—he got away from us and ran."

"The prisoner?" I echoed and scratched my head. Against all common sense, I was enjoying his company (I rarely spoke to anyone other than my brother); besides, we were both "professionals," after a fashion, and there was no harm in a bit of conversational sport, a mood game to be played out of the sight of the citizenry.

"Well, I did *hear* something," I lied, and then the man looked pleased, and I was pleased.

"It was a sound like chains in a box," I said, immediately regretting it.

"What are you talking about?" he said, and then he gave me another long look and seemed to think he understood something about me, something he had missed at first, and he turned without another word and left.

I went back to stealing gunpowder, looked forward to the day when I would see his body piled among the others.

Ben

Ben watched her every move. It was still raining outside. The fire, orange and pleasantly shapeless, burned in the fireplace; the warmth hit his knees, drying out his pale trousers. Each pop of the wood as the fire ignited deposits of sap was a declaration of his happiness. Her youth and her seriousness. The blackness of her hair. The smell of wood burning. The milk cascading from the cold metal pitcher into her cup. The roundness of her gestures, the abundance of milk. Probably, he would have to leave as soon as the storm passed. She was so kind! Perhaps out of kindness, she tolerated him. That morning, she must have stretched in bed without self-consciousness, sighing awake beneath the light sheet. Ben imagined leaning over her, touching the edge of the counterpane as he stood dizzily within the inner chamber.

"Cookie?" she said. She held out a silver tray of cookies, rare and diverse, as if collected from the world's most remote territories: pulled from the soft, ridged ocean floor, plucked from the canopy of misty trees. One cookie was a cylinder of thin pastry, perfectly burned around the edges, as if shaved from a tree with a hot sword. His hand hovered over the tray. He worried that she was getting tired of holding the tray. But how could he think clearly in the presence of this insane splendor?

"They are all so beautiful," he said quietly. He lifted the cylinder cookie gently. "Thank you." He didn't know whether to eat or to breathe. His heart ached in her presence, or in the presence of the cookies. The rain picked up, gusting against the windows. Rainwater gushed from the gutters, overflowing them. Was there anything as thrilling as the motherly concern of intelligent women?

"It's like we're behind a waterfall," he said, unable to stop smiling.

"It's quite a storm," she said.

Ben could see the future: on the kitchen counter, we'll always keep some fresh fruit in a walnut bowl, fruit from our own trees—limes, apples, clementines. And if a tree stops bearing fruit and dies, I'll cut it up for firewood on the chopping block, deep in the yard. I'll haul the columns of wood onto the block, and I'll split them with all my strength, and then bury the blade of my ax in the chopping block so it can do no harm.

Ben sighed, contented in his thoughts. As long as the storm continued, the future stretched out before him. Yet, for her, he considered, this is perhaps merely the enactment of a good deed. He reminded himself: this was not an open-ended hour, one in which he could safely search forever for the word or words that would explain everything.

"Yes," he said, "a rain like this may never stop."

"It can seem that way," she agreed.

Ben scanned the room for conversation. He couldn't think of where to start. He thought: there should be children running in the yard, happily wild, while he chopped the wood; fearless, loud children who would call out to the neighbors (*Watch out! There's father! He's chopping!*). Or he might be the father of shy, sweet children who would fall silent when strangers walked into the yard, a boy and a girl who would cling to his legs and hide their faces. Ben sighed. I will lay my hands upon their soft heads, and I will smile neighborly at the peaceful stranger, and you will be beside me, and you will be the one with whom I share the observations. *The flowers are beautiful this spring*, I will probably say, or I will pull an apple from the apple tree thriving in our yard and halve the apple gently on the chopping block, while summer light seeps into our brains.

"May I have another cookie?"

"Of course," she said and again held the tray for him.

Ben reconsidered the diversity of the cookies on the platter—more than one man could ever hope to eat alone. Am I one of many, and not just many, but very, very many? She had eaten none of the cookies herself. Ben took the silver tray and held it for her. "Cookie?" he asked.

"Oh, no, thank you," she said. She leaned toward Ben, as if to tell him a secret. *Pop!* A pocket of sap burst in the log. *Pop!*

"So violent," she said thoughtfully and leaned back.

"Yes, it's quite a downpour," Ben said, holding the tray.

"Oh, I mean the fire."

"Hmm." Ben paused, summoning nonchalance. "Do you have a special connection to a baker or something?"

"Hardly," she said. "I'll tell you a secret: I hate cookies. And everything sweet."

Ben put down the tray and frowned at it. "I'm sorry."

"Please, don't be," she said.

The grandfather clock behind her was ticking off thin, quick paces behind its blank face. Ben lifted the pale fabric of his pants away from his legs; his knees were uncomfortably hot. The rain was letting up, sunlight invading the gray comfort of the room. She reached for his cup and carried it to the sideboard. He watched her back as she poured the tea. A bowl of oranges was on the marble tabletop, a loose stack of fresh orange peels beside it; Ben imagined the smell of oranges on her fingertips as she poured tea into his cup. She spoke over her shoulder, as if they knew one another. "It's looking better outside," she said brightly. Ben could hear the clink of the spoon as she dropped it on the marble tabletop.

In the late afternoon or early evening, around an outdoor table, you and I will bat away the sweet little bees with our hands, never slackening our conversation, and I will wear my light wool sweater when I rake the yard of autumn leaves. (She brought him his tea and sat down again across from him.) He and she would never become restless or uneasy—the crackling fireplace in wintertime would drain them of uncomfortable appetites and strengthen their aptitude for daily life, and the ice would tighten upon the eaves in their sleep, and they would wake to the sight of bright red berries, alive and capped in snow. The sky will be powder-white or powder-blue or charcoal-gray with rain, and we'll pull the static sweaters over the heads of healthy, happy children who smell of clean and ice-cold air.

Ben leaned toward her and whispered, "You don't like cookies, and I don't like to hunt."

"And here we are," she said conspiratorially and winked.

"How have we ended up—"

"Ended up here together?" she offered.

"Yes," said Ben, uncertainly. "Together."

"*Marooned together?*"

"Um. I don't know about—"

"*Marooned together, yet we need only to say something different, and to listen to one another.* It's from an old poem."

"Ancestors' Poem?"

"No, no. Something I wrote a long time ago."

"Oh," said Ben, taking note of his mild confusion, which he knew could be a sign of love. "I love poetry, which of course most bachelors don't. And, I mean, I paint, paint paintings."

"I *love* that," she said. "What do you paint?"

"Still lifes. Mostly fruits."

"Huh."

"I also paint others things," he added quickly, thinking of Finton's work. "A man on an island, surrounded only by horses. Marooned, in fact."

She smiled and said, "Exactly."

He reached for her hand across the shallow table between them. There was a loud rapping on the windowpane. Ben jumped; the young woman jumped. An old man in a sky-blue sweater tapped the glass with the barrel of a shotgun.

"Shit," she said. "My father."

Ben leaned back, frowning.

"When you come back, find me," she said.

"I will."

"I'll be walking in the orchard behind the house—come find me. We have a lot to talk about."

The father had disappeared from the window. Ben stood and took his hat from the hearth, where she had hung it carefully to dry upon a hot hook driven into the dark wood of the mantel. The silk lining had become quite hot. He pulled it ruthlessly down onto his head. It had tightened in the heat, and he could feel a headache forming over his eyes almost instantly. The silk band burned his forehead: an excellent simulation of a fever. It would have to do for now.

He turned again to face her, just as the father stormed into the room. "Young man!" he said.

The air was cool and thick with fog. "My hat's damp," complained one of the bachelors, flicking the brim of his hat. "We've drifted far out to sea," joked another, as he blew into the embers of a low campfire. The father had brought Ben out among the young men hunting and put a rifle in his hands. "Fucking fathers," said one of the other men sympathetically, lifting his rifle to take aim at the father's back as he walked back toward the house. "That motherfucker brought me out here yesterday," said the man as he brought his rifle back down, "when he caught me waving at her across the yard."

"She made me tea," said Ben gleefully. "Then she gave me cookies."

The other bachelor leveled his rifle at Ben's head. "Keep talking!"

"Oh, shut up, you two, why don't you? Just enjoy a little sport in support of the real sport—a bit of shooting and then back up to the house."

The bachelor lowered his gun but continued to stare at
Ben. "Where are you from?"

"From?" Ben asked innocently.

"You look familiar to me."

Ben shrugged, yanked his hat lower. He turned to study
the fog. Occasionally it cleared, and he glimpsed acres of
grayish-green fields splayed before them, the earth broken
into rectangles by rock walls and rows of weeds. Everything
else shorn. The fog rolled in again, hiding the countryside.
The other men sat in a circle on the damp ground and
played cards sullenly, their rifles across their laps. "Damn
this fog," said one of the men and pressed his hand over his
eyes. "You all right there, buddy?"

"Of course I'm all right," said the man and glared at him
with cold eyes. "I'm just listening. Someone should tell a
story."

"Do you know the story of Captain Meeks and the
Corporal?" asked a slim bachelor, very young.

"We have heard it, but it feels good to remember," said
the bachelors in flat unison and fell quiet.

"This all happened a long time ago, when the Enemy
was after the heart of the city. It's easy to forget that our
beloved city park was once a battlefield and that the blood
of our brothers was shed there. We should be grateful for
their sacrifices."

"We are grateful for them."

"Captain Meeks was still a young soldier, stationed
on the Near Ridge. He was fearless and full of love for the
city, a love that was so strong, it sometimes forced him to
sit suddenly upon a rock to rest his heart, even in the heat
of battle. This is why we say a man may have 'a Captain's
Heart.'" Ben pulled his hat low over his face: the agony of
the forced march.

"One day, the Corporal joined their unit, and it fell upon the Captain to protect and to care for him. The Corporal was not an ordinary man, and neither was the Captain, but we must never forget that they once walked on the earth no differently than you or I."

"We should strive to be better."

"The Corporal had arrived wrapped in his tight, pale sheet, his head exposed, his deep, dark eyes endlessly staring. The Captain was in awe of him. The Corporal *knew* everything, had *seen* everything, had *heard* everything, and he understood the Enemy better than the Enemy understood himself. The Corporal was famous even then for making his rounds, carried from camp to camp, and wherever he went, he inspired men, and the Great Fight was redoubled, and the Enemy fell back.

"The Captain watched over the Corporal as he lay on the ground, still as a corpse and quiet as a saint, and waited. The Corporal was listening to the Enemy's mind. When he felt the Enemy's thoughts turning toward the city, the Corporal let out a piercing cry from the heart of the camp: the birds would explode from the tops of the green trees, and the animals hunting each other innocently in the shadows would freeze, and the men would roll terrified from their rustasacks and stomp out the low fire and aim their rifles into the trees, and they knew the Enemy was almost upon them. They were listening. The Corporal was teaching them to listen and to understand.

"The men became so attuned to the Corporal that any sound—a sigh, a sudden breath—might cause them to panic, to roll from their rustasacks and to run screaming from an invisible terror, and Captain Meeks, eternally the master of his feelings, would tackle the men and hold them in the mud until they had become calm again. *Be quiet,*

Captain Meeks would say, and they were quiet."

"Yes, be quiet," Ben said under his breath.

The storyteller seemed to emerge from a trance. He surveyed his surroundings, and his eyes fell on Ben, and he said, "I'm sorry? You said something?" The other men turned to study Ben, and he saw the angry bachelor shift his rifle casually in Ben's direction.

"The Captain said it, and so it would be so, Brother," Ben added quickly.

"Yes, it *was* so. While his men played cards, the Captain would sit in the dark with the Corporal and hand-feed him his own rations and sleep beside him in the dirt in order to keep the soldiers from pouring great quantities of black-market liquor down the Corporal's throat, as they sometimes did in an effort to get the Corporal to stop listening.

"One night, the Captain lay beside the Corporal and considered their camp—the gray stubs of felled trees, the pockmarked rocks, dinged by bored soldiers' gunshots, charred logs, old food tins, ruined boots, and down in the harbor, burned-out ships drifting . . . disorder among men, disorder and fear of what might come. The Corporal was an old, old soldier, and that night, the Captain realized that the Corporal had mastered a new state, enviable and intermediate: he was both destroyed and whole.

"The Captain wanted to make this world a better place. He wanted to be unafraid, and to listen to what was hard to hear, and to look upon what was hard to see. He tugged at the pale sheet in which the Corporal was bundled, and the Corporal stared back at him with large, silent eyes and seemed to understand. The Captain lowered the sheet gently, inch by inch, until he could see the Corporal's naked body in the moonlight. It was marked with deep, dark scars, and the Captain reached down and touched a black hole of burned flesh in the Corporal's chest, and he was not afraid. Now he understood what the Corporal had endured, what he had lost. The Corporal suddenly lifted one of his bone-thin arms and hooked it around the Captain's neck. The Corporal was strong and his grip was merciless, and he pulled the Captain's face to his lips and said, 'A man did this to me.' The Captain listened. The Corporal said, 'Shall I tell you a story? If I do, you and I can never part.'"

The men were silent. Ben's eyes filled with tears—he hated how the old tales moved him, in spite of his hatred of them. One of the bachelors jumped up and tackled Ben, pinning him to the ground and hissing into his ear, "Shall I tell you a story? If I do . . ."

"Show some respect!" said Ben and struggled to his feet and looked wildly at his jacket sleeves, now black with mud. "I'm covered in mud!"

"No harm meant, Brother."

"Selfridge!" said the angry bachelor. "Do you know Selfridge?"

"Selfridge?"

"Selfridge. That's how I recognize you. Selfridge told me all about you. See you got your suit."

Ben was trying to calculate what the angry man might know and what it would mean. "Yes," said Ben, "finally got my suit from the tailor."

"Kind of a loose fit, isn't it?"

"Quiet, you two. Listen," interrupted one of the others.

Ben held his rifle loosely in one hand and listened carefully. He heard the shouts of men somewhere in the fog. The bachelor beside him raised his gun and scanned the fog. "Don't shoot," said Ben, "There are people there." Ben strained to see into the thick, milky air; he could hear voices, people running; the bachelor fired. *Pop! Pop! Pop!* "Don't shoot!" Objects were falling out of the sky, fluttering to the ground. His first thought was, *books?* "Got it!" shouted the man at his side. Ben heard more shots, saw the bank of fog light up with bursts of orange light, and then he made out the shape of another bachelor: his pale suit ghostly in the thick fog, he was a floating head, floating hands. He was aiming his rifle at Ben.

"No! Don't shoot!" He tried to run, but he was frozen to spot, his legs pooling with cold blood. The bachelor held Ben in his sights and fired, slamming Ben to the ground.

Ben watched the gently sloped hills in the distance: the fog clung to them. An etherizing cotton. Foxes and rabbits and birds felt nothing when they fell, wounded, onto the soft bank of etherizing cotton. Ben felt better, calmer. The hole in his chest pulsed blood. Ben tried to slow his heart, to keep the blood in his veins. Blood was spreading along the fibers of his pale jacket, almost entirely red and wet. There was the tableau of ashen-faced men standing over him, their gray hats pushed back on their heads.

Other men emerged from the fog; one man had a dead bird by the neck. Ben's face felt hot, his feet dirt cold. A man knelt beside him. "You'll be all right, Brother." The death words, the man was speaking the death words. Ben tried to shake his head. *No, no, no.* "Looks like we've had a bit of an accident," said the hateful bachelor and smiled.

Ben pressed his cheek against the muddy moss of the ground to cool his head, a place that was becoming unbearable. He could see the house and orchard behind it. The fog rolled forward again, devouring the muddy shoes of the hunters.

When Ben came to again, he was wrapped in a bedsheet; men were hustling him back to the house. He had been dreaming about the sound of the bell of the knife grinder's cart in the rain, when the knife grinder parked his cart at his mother's house and rang his copper bell. Ben loved that sound. When it rained, the knife grinder would pull his cart under the eaves of the house and work behind a little waterfall as the water overflowed the gutters. His mother would take down her heaviest sewing scissors, and the knife grinder would sharpen the blades, pumping the wheel faster and faster, sending yellow and orange sparks shooting into the yard, and his mother would ring the bell in a funny way to cheer Ben up, since he had no father.

Meeks

I was pacing outside the station, as I did most afternoons now, waiting impatiently for Bedge to clear my name and for my life to resume its normal shape, when I saw a figure walking between the fog-washed trees of the park path and approaching the station. He moved nimbly, as the energetic elderly often do, and, without thinking, I hid myself behind the work shed and peeked out in time to see his back: he was wearing a well-tailored black jacket. He pulled open the massive door of the station and went in. The great door swung shut behind him.

I spent some time reconstituting the scene using the particulars: I had only seen his back, but there was something about the small head that reminded me . . . and there was the black jacket. I didn't want to importune Bedge more than I already had, but at last I was persuaded that I had seen what I had seen, and I climbed the steps to the station and yanked at the door. It wouldn't budge.

Had they locked me out? Had I become weak beyond

belief? I kicked at the door with all my strength, and I called his name: *Bedge! Bedge!*

A long time went by. Bedge finally appeared on the station steps, unrolling his sleeves and buttoning the cuffs. Bedge! I said breathlessly, and he was startled.

What are you doing here, Meeks?

You've found him? Is he inside now?

At last, he said, No, Meeks. It was an actor.

An actor?

I'm interviewing actors for the Independence Day plays, that's all. He's just an actor.

My thoughts fell into disarray; I stared; I was failing to react to circumstances so alien to my hopes.

Bedge sat on the top step. Come have a talk with me, he said.

I settled beside Bedge on the top step; I considered the blows of distant hammers. At the edge of the park, I could see workmen uncoiling and checking lengths of theatrical rope, dredging the shortest lengths in a trough of boiling tar. The air was cool and coppery with the low clouds of autumnal leaves upon the trees.

Bedge put his arm around me. Would you like a mint? he asked.

I said I would, and he handed me a mint. I unwrapped it and inspected the stamped city seal, the iconography of which I'd never been able to decipher, despite a lifetime of study.

Bedge, I said, what does this look like to you? (I saw a human heart crossed by shafts of wheat.)

Bedge tightened his grip on my shoulder and said, *Meeks, Meeks, Meeks.*

In my experience, this kind of wistful repetition of a word tends to signal a change and is rarely insignificant.

Bedge reached over and took my hand, the one that I had injured. How is your hand? he asked.

Much better, I said and flexed it open and closed to show him.

He held my hand tenderly. I had known him for most of my life.

All of these actors are disasters, he confided in me.

I smiled knowingly. I had seen my share of dissolute actors. There was a temporary silence between us, entirely comfortable; I felt my body relax into his. He patted my wounded hand.

How would you like a role? A part in one of the plays?

I sat in stunned silence. A *part*? I finally managed.

Yes, said Bedge; he stood abruptly and descended the stairs. He looked up at me.

Yes! I said. Anything.

Something in the Lovers Play?

No, thank you, I said, and blushed, yanking reflexively at my immovable cap.

Bedge was suddenly very cheerful—it seemed that he, too, was a victim of the mirth of the holiday season.

The Founders Play, I said. Captain Meeks, I added, emboldened by his good mood.

I sat for a long time on the steps of the police station, stayed long after Bedge had gone back inside to work. I was in very high spirits, almost uncomfortably so. I wished I had someone to whom I could give my good news—such extreme joy, kept to oneself, can be as burdensome as a terrible secret.

Postcards littered the ground at my feet. I used the tip of my boot to pull a few into view. Pictures of the fat black cliffs of remote lands, the tufted crowns of foreign trees leaning far out over the dark water in search of sunlight. Pictures of the gouged-out soft green moss of other peoples' valleys, vistas, fields. Pictures of the frail, wind-torqued houses in which strangers were living, living horribly. The frowning shepherds in the gray fields wherein the unquarried stone was sleeping—we came for it! We made it live. Reed-thin farmers, skeletal cows, doomed goats, but God is just. This city is weaned on tales of terror, tales of the Enemy's galloping horses, their big-headed and mean cats, their devious smiling dogs, their untrustworthy children, their lonely, fat wives, their tall, competent friends, their homicidal surgeons, their unpredictable soldiers . . . yet the Enemy's world looked like a grave: the degradation of a story causes the degradation of the land, of the body; the wrong words can corrode the living world, verily, verily. I leaned down and sifted through the cards at my feet and picked one, an old-fashioned postcard of the Enemy's Territory: the forest still flush and green with unfamiliar trees, the grid of fishing nets smooth upon the water, the full white sails of anachronistic ships mirroring full-bellied beautiful clouds overhead. This postcard was forbidden, of course; it was, in fact, my job as a policeman to prevent it from being in the park in the first place. Yet, I could only think, How beautiful, how beautiful . . .

My mother had told me a few secrets about the past, about the place from which she had come, stories that she used to whisper to me and to me alone, "And in those days, long ago, in the place whence we came . . ." she used to say. I pocketed the card guiltily, my face hot.

Ben

He had found his mother standing in the front hall of the old house holding a postcard, the front door hanging open;

the expression on her face seemed to cast the whole house in a dangerous, alien light. Ben waited, frightened. On the postcard, he could see the rolling white surf and leaning trees of foreign shores. "Your father's not coming home," she said.

One morning that spring, his mother woke him before dawn and told him to pack.

"We're going to find your father," she said cheerfully and tousled his hair. "We're going to one of the islands, right to the edge of the sea!"

"Is he there?" Ben felt sick with terror and hope. He could smell the cakes cooling in the baker's window; he could hear the long blast of the ferry's horn.

"We better hurry. Pack your things, Ben."

His mother stood stiffly at the railing on the ferry, peering into the water where the bow sliced it into wakes.

"Is it far away?" asked Ben, but his mother didn't seem to hear him. He watched her carefully, or watched the sea-birds hover over the blue-gray water, eyeing the shadows of their victims sliding obliviously. Ben watched them, or he watched the lavender horizon, the widening band of the atmosphere over their destination. The whole azure: happiness assured! His father would be standing on the beach, or ankle deep in the surf. *Ben! My dear! I see you got my postcard.*

Ben and his mother walked across a crooked gangway onto shore, the unfamiliar tufts of orange and pale-green flower, the shoreline nests of frothing water. They passed through an open archway into the lobby of the whitewashed hotel. They had walked up a thousand steps, possibly ten thousand,

and his mother had dragged a suitcase up the steps behind her, leaving Ben to drag the other, though he was a small boy. Their arms were trembling when they arrived at the front desk. Men soaked in salt water dripped through the lobby, holding sardines bound through the gills on rounds of twine. "That's dinner," said the smiling woman behind the desk. Ben stood on the veranda and looked out over the water while his mother negotiated, the sharp white waves threshing the surface of the sea.

Ben and his mother unpacked, rested confusedly on the salt-stale cushions of the tourist chairs. Ben put on his bathing suit and waited on the steps.

"Go ahead," she said, "but be careful."

Ben ran down the beach and into the water; a powerful wave rolled over him, pinning him to the sand, sucking him seaward. He crawled out of the water and collapsed on the crust of dry, white sand; behind him were the charred remains of former beach fires, ash dusted the pale sand. He smelled the narrow, speckled fish cooking, spiked on sharpened sticks stabbed deep into the sand beside small fires, blazes of yellow-orange flower. Beached jellyfish were thick lenses upon the sand. His mother brought him a mango; he peeled away the skin inexpertly; he bit into the sweet sherbet-colored fruit; he scraped the hard pit with his teeth. He buried the pit in the sand and rinsed his hands in the seawater. He followed the paranoid, supercilious crabs from wet rock to wet rock. He stared down the long, narrow, speckled fish that gathered in the tidal pools when the tide went out, the fish all facing forward dourly like parishioners in the cool cathedral space between the jetty rocks.

Local boys ran out of the water holding octopuses away from their bodies, octopus arms clinging to boy arms with fleshy, sucking cups; boys walked out of the water with spears or nets, catching their breath, silver water pouring from their dark, thick hair. They hauled their catches to the hotel porch, where cooks gutted and cleaned the fish while the boys rested in the heat, plucking fruit from the trees that lined the grassy alleys between the houses. Ben looked on enviously. His fear was boyish; the fearlessness of other boys looked holy. The boys crashed back into the water to hunt.

Ben went into the hotel, searching for his mother. He walked through the dining room, past hotel guests squeezing lemon wedges over their grilled fish. He checked their room; everything seemed sad—sad towels, sad bags, sad shoes—after the bright, windy crowds on the beach. He found her on the veranda and stretched out beside her on a wicker couch, resting his head in her lap, and fell asleep listening to waves. He woke to the sound of his mother arguing with a man from the hotel.

"My husband was a casualty of the war. And his widow and his son are entitled to be here."

"No, madam. It is not the same thing."

"My husband—the boy's father—was lost to the war."

"Madam, it was not at the hands of the Enemy."

"Where is this famous Enemy of yours?"

"Madam?"

Ben and his mother packed hastily, boarded the ferry, and stood on the deck, looking toward home. He heard the motor's drone, caught the nauseating smell of burning oil as swells lifted the chugging motor out of the water and made it cough black smoke, the cabin door swinging open and slamming shut, the gray marbleizing lift of the current, the white, foamy lift unevening the ship. The empty horizon unreachable and bland, tilting in the rough water. Ben clung to the railing, feeling sick. He glared at the ferry captain who was smoking and daydreaming in his cramped glass booth, rolling them into wave after wave.

"Mother?"

"Not now, Ben."

Meeks

The gun seemed to be biting or stinging me in the ribs, perhaps because it could detect a change in my heart: I was in love with this world again. I stopped in the shade of a river tree and peered carefully into my coat—there it was, the same as ever, sleeping in its corner.

I went to see my mother, who, naturally, remains underground. Nonetheless, I told her my wonderful news. Mother, I whispered, you are hearing the voice of Captain Meeks. Not your son, Meeks, but the Captain himself. Mother, I'm *in* the play.

I held my breath—perhaps I was waiting, however unconsciously, for some kind of reply. Then again, I suspect my mother had always known this day would come. My head was aching—I tried pointlessly to loosen the police hat's grip with my fingertips. I had never spent an Independence Day without her. We used to sit together on our favorite rock, well removed from the crowds, and wait for the Lovers Play to begin.

This is all real, I would say to her, and I would point to the flat rock upon which we were sitting, and to the ivy at our feet. That, I said, pointing to the stage, is *not*. Mother smiled at my observation; the play commenced. She sat on the flat rock; I stood behind her on my toes, straining to see over the audience, steadying myself by placing my hands on her shoulders. Workers sat in the branches of the great tree and managed the theatrical ropes, lowering the curtain, setting counterfeit storms in motion, lifting actors off their feet so they could appear to ascend or to suddenly drop. I watched a pair of brothers arguing on a high branch, one grabbing at the rope the other was holding, the other shushing his brother furiously. I laughed at this ancillary and unofficial bit of comedy taking place above the main action. Hearing me laugh, my mother reached back and took one of my hands so that she could press it against her cheek.

On the stage sat a pair of lovers; an ancient estate loomed behind them. I was a boy, and I was with my mother, and some actors were enacting a play in the park. I sighed with contentment. A thin and silvery veil fell behind the lovers, as if the enormous house had been cast backward into a fog. The lovers leaned in close but were startled apart again by the distant pops of hunting rifles, and the screen shot back up into the trees, and the house in the background suddenly loomed large—the father charged from the wings, storming across the stage.

I buried my face in my mother's thick, dark hair and covered my ears. Of course, I knew things would turn out well for the lovers even then, but the certainty of the outcome seemed to have no bearing on my fear as I waited for the lovers to be united in the final scene, in the glow of a wedding feast, and, concurrently, all of the new marriages of all the couples in the audience were solemnized. Happiness engineered to function on a massive scale. Who could doubt the genius of the Captain?

The sets were cleared; people milled about, entertaining themselves with fresh critiques of the familiar tale. They spread blankets out on the grass and lay about in their sweaters, and new wives fed new husbands figs, and fathers sawed salami discs for children to gnaw, and the workers, too, lay about in large numbers, chatting quietly to one another or sleeping in the gentle autumnal sunshine. Mother and I watched contentedly from our rock.

The crowd reassembled for the Founders Play. Couples huddled together against the chill in the air and watched the stage intently. I sat very still in my mother's lap, and even the birds fell into penitent and tense silence as they watched.

The old Police Chief climbed the steps. Workers walked in pairs on either side of the cake, carrying lengths of burning rope low over the surface to light the multitude of candles. Then the people began to chant: *Meeks! Meeks! Meeks!* My mother and I smiled at one another, at the deliciousness of our situation.

Do you hear that? she said.

They're calling me!

You must not go, she said and held me and refused to let go.

I would pretend to struggle. Finally she would let me stand, and I would point to the platform. Mother, I would say, you must understand that I must go, because the people need me.

Then she would bury her face in her hands and pretend to weep, and though her weeping (and, may I say, her acting in general) was utterly unconvincing and couldn't have fooled a child, I could never withstand this spectacle, and I would break character immediately to run to her side and pry away her hands in order to see her face and say, Mother, are you really crying?

Then she would pull me back into her lap, and we would watch the rest of the play together. This is real, said my mother reassuringly, as she pressed my hand against the cool, smooth surface of the rock. And that, she said pointing to the stage, is *not*. Only then could I relax into enjoyment of the final scene: the Bell Ringer took hold of the rope and yanked it hard, sending the Condemned Man flying through the trap door. The enemy of all our hopes was hanged! Or, I should say, the actors had made it seem so, and the *bom, bom, bom* of the evening bells rolled over the city in triumph.

Mother and I would make our way eventually to the heart of the action, where people were cutting greedily into the Independence Day cake, using the knives they had brought from home, and everyone partook of the cake, including Mother and me, and while the other families headed home to boisterous dinners around a centerpiece that was both a page from the history of our world as well as a piece of cake, Mother and I would stay in the park, surrounded by the trampled effects of a massive celebration. Another Independence Day, Mother sighed, as we ghosted past the empty stage or watched the theater workers coil the ropes and begin the sweeping away of the evidence of the day. The remains . . . through which Mother and I wandered in a mother-and-son melancholy that I loved. Though this division from others suited me perfectly when I was a boy, I hated the way in which, invariably, it cut into my mother's mood. The people headed home. Mother and I sat in the park. I ate and ate, while Mother left her cake untouched and watched the workers clear the park.

Ben

He kicked away the heavy blankets. Blood had seeped through the outer layer of bandaging around his chest. He tried to think of something nice. He wished his father were alive to witness the beautiful symmetry of their lives. The last day he spent with his father, they had gone to the park. His father said nothing, picked through a box of blueberries. Ben heard a low pop, then a surge: the long rows of old-fashioned lamps lining the walk were glowing to life. Ben's father stared thoughtfully into the box of blueberries, and handed one to Ben.

"Do blueberries grow on trees? Do they start as flowers?"

His father raised a finger to his lips and said, "Shhhh."

It was early evening in the late summer, and the park lights were glowing like campfires yellow in a fog. Ben placed the blueberry reverently on his tongue, and then crushed it against the roof of his mouth. He remembered the comforting dim glow of fresh lemons on the nearby fruit cart, the spiked fruits from far away, snug in their paper-box compartments like saints' relics, the green-tinged bananas, as if tinged with green smoke. The pyramids of red, polished apples and the rock-gray potatoes in the crates under the fruit stand: his heaven and earth. How had they all come into this world? These and all the other things he thought of as his. How would he coax them back into existence if he were charged with replicating life, with repeating the signs of creation he had always seen and heard? If this world were destroyed tomorrow, if the Enemy crossed the river at night and laid the universe of his boyhood bare? He wouldn't even know which things to put on the trees, which in the sea, which he would hide underground for the farmers to yank free.

Ben heard a shoe scuff the floor on the other side of the bedroom door; he heard a truck start laboriously and then idle; he heard the house pipes filling up with water; Ben heard the birds whistling cautiously outside his window.

A door slammed shut deep inside the house; Ben recognized the sharp outline of a porcelain pitcher on an antique table beneath the bright window. (He loved her! He loved her!)

The doctor and the young woman's father carried Ben, wrapped in his bedsheets, from the house. It was night; it was cool out; the father kicked the car door shut. Soon the unmistakable sounds of the city were upon them. Ben woke up in the old hospital beneath the low ceiling of the basement ward. Surgeons, Brothers of Mercy, dying men, and, somewhere in the great building, Ben considered, laboring mothers at work on the creation of new Brothers and Sisters. Ben lay in bed and thought about the young woman, alone in the dead quiet of the country estate, every pleasure hobbled, he hoped, by her regret. Why had she let him go?

One afternoon, the Brothers of Mercy came onto the ward. Ben could smell the acrid bite of their boot polish, the childlike sweetness of their talcum-dusted bodies. One of the doctors pointed at Ben in his hospital bed; he was sitting against his pillow sketching a mango on a notepad the Brothers of Mercy had given him.

A pair of Brothers stopped by his bed. "You're looking better, old man!" said one. Ben smiled noncommittally. One Brother fished a pair of rumpled dark trousers from a sack; the other Brother threw a gray smock across Ben's chest.

Ben was wearing the gray smock, sitting by the river in the oblique autumn sun. His pale suit had been shredded by an idiot country doctor obsessed with finding secondary wounds. His beautiful suit destroyed, the suit that had made him *him*. And he had lost her. How?

Yellow jackets drifted from the head of a neglected statue by the water. The yellow jackets floated evilly between the rusted spikes of the statue's crown. Her sword was pointed toward the ground; the blade disappeared into the high weeds; her broad, strong hands rested coolly on the massive hilt. She and Ben were looking out over the river, and beyond the river to the open sea! The Brothers of Mercy were watching Ben closely; he dug dutifully in his suit pocket for his lunch, though he had no appetite. He unwrapped one of the stale pastries the doctor had given him. He licked the powdered sugar from the sides. Other men talked, smoked behind the mangy river trees, coursed back and forth through the tree shadows. The Brothers of Mercy watched everything. Yellow jackets descended behind the sharp points of the statue's crown and disappeared; there must be a seasonal nest living in the head of the statue, thought Ben. The unimaginable state of her mind! For the yellow jackets, for her, for him, it was near the end—the days were growing cold and small.

Ben broke off a small piece of pastry and then bit the piece in half. He wished it were possible to keep things— the granite pinks of the autumn sky, the charred pilings of the collapsed piers, the sugar on his tongue—permanent and vivid without compressing them into memories. He wrapped the pastry in the worn piece of wax paper and shoved it deep into his pocket. The strong autumnal sun hit his face; cool air was rushing in from the river.

"Back on your feet! Move it!" One of the Brothers was poking at Ben's legs with a stick.

Meeks

Bedge had instructed me to meet him at the station the day before the big day. As I walked toward the station, I liked to think I was indistinguishable from the many energetic walkers and friendly nodders and other purposeful souls who characterize our city, especially during the holidays. I strode with great purpose, and I bounded up the steps to the police station; I opened the door effortlessly and went inside.

Bedge took me into the room at the end of the hall—a small, plain room dominated by an enormous table and a few chairs lining the wall. Black jackets had been hung over the backs of several of the empty chairs. Seated in one of the chairs was a diminutive older man with a measuring tape draped around his neck. The little man sat upright, with his hands settled equidistantly on his knees—his whole being seemed to be in a state of careful apprehension. Bedge, he said quickly and stood. I felt that Bedge and I were old friends suddenly in the presence of an awkward and unfortunate outsider.

This is the tailor, said Bedge—he had ignored the tailor's greeting. He'll fit you for your suit—your costume.

The tailor approached me, holding his measuring tape out like a net, as if I were some simple creature who could be crept up on and captured. I backed away and glanced at Bedge. I was wary of the tailor and do not, as a rule, enjoy or find easy to tolerate the touch of strangers' hands upon my body, even upon my clothes. Sensing my dis-ease, Bedge added, it's just the jacket. Your pants are dark enough and will do. (I looked down at my pants—they were almost black with filth.)

The tailor waited, his measuring tape slack in his hands.

He said, Spread your arms out like this, and he demonstrated for me.

I stood still, my arms extended to the sides. I stared into the thick glass of the window. I could make out the faint vertical lines of the bars on the other side. The tailor opened a black case on the table; I peeked over my shoulder and surveyed the contents—they might easily be mistaken for instruments of torture: boxes of glinting metal pins, blades, the hard mouths of black clips, small and giant pairs of scissors.

The tailor removed my coat, an operation during which I flinched repeatedly. I stood miserably, vulnerable as a naked child; I crossed my arms over my chest.

Oh, my God. What's this? said the tailor, feeling the outline of the gun hidden in the lining of my jacket. He has a gun!

The tailor rushed to Bedge and grabbed at his shirt, as if he intended to yank open the doors to his barrel chest and hide there. I stayed where I was, humbled by the revelation of my lies upon lies in Bedge's eyes, but when the tailor turned, I could see that he was genuinely frightened: I was a deranged animal, long-tortured and held back only by a rusted circus chain—but he was an innocent man! He handed the jacket to Bedge: Here, you can feel it. It's definitely a gun.

Please step away from me immediately, said Bedge, glaring at the tailor. Bedge refused to look at me, studied the gun. It's empty, he said. Not even loaded. Now, shall we proceed?

That's it? said the tailor, backing away. That's all you're going to say?

Bedge questioned me: Meeks, where did this come from?

From the man I arrested in the park, I said, staring at my boots.

As I suspected. Were you intending to hurt anyone with it?

No! I was only thinking of the man in the black jacket.

Of course you were. Will you let me take care of him?

I'm sorry, Bedge.

It's OK. Now, put your arms out like this, said Bedge, extending his arms. I stared at him, imitated him. Bedge pointed at the tailor's chest—*Finish* your work!—and then sat down in one of the chairs lining the wall. The tailor had me try on a few jackets, and then busied himself around my body, circling me like a stable fly, nipping fabric here and there. I stared straight ahead, my heart pounding impatiently in my chest. As he made adjustments, the tailor rambled on about the state of the city, the fine work of the police, the decline of certain streets, the importance of guiding the young, the detestable strangeness of people new to this neighborhood or that. I looked to Bedge once or twice for reassurance, but he gazed past me, as if he were sitting alone in the room and remembering someone fondly—I liked to think it was me he was remembering.

The tailor angled pins speedily through the seams of the jacket hanging on my body and went on excitedly: I mean, consider the cake this year: It has never been longer or better; never have there been more people at work on it; the vibrancy of the icing is a revelation. . . . Bedge stared, said nothing; I lost track of time. The next thing I knew, I was bristling with pins, and my arms were growing weak from the effort of holding them up, and the tailor was snapping shut his case.

The tailor tried to remove the pinned jacket, and I balked. He snorted derisively at my fear. It's just a jacket! I knew rationally, or I had persuaded myself over the years to accept, that certain feelings and ideas, not to mention other internal phenomena, were merely the indigenous creatures of my head who had no real jurisdiction in the real world, whose rages were harmless to outsiders and whose fears were rooted in nothing, but they were all I had, and so I listened.

Ben

The factory buildings loomed like the hulls of warships lined up on the horizon. Municipal banners snapped against the line, slack as sheets and then taut as sails. Thick white clouds spewed from the narrow stacks, dimming the bright yellow lights of the factory behind drifts of smoke. The Brothers of Mercy marched Ben and the other men through the factory gates and into the industrial courtyard. Ben stopped to try to catch his breath. His progress was slow; two of the Brothers stayed behind with him, jabbing him occasionally with a stick, goading him down the buckled asphalt path. The smell of burning or boiling tar filled the courtyard; dying beetles spun through the air, crashing headlong into the dry grass on either side of the main path. The towering windows of the factory were the ramparts of empires of light. Love and dread: the mysterious familiar finally met.

The Brothers shoved and shouted, moving Ben and the other men through the long, loud rooms of the mint factory. Past boiling vats, past pale sacks packed with powdered tints (yellow, red, blue), past undernourished-looking men running mints through machines that stamped them with the municipal seal (a hunk of precious ore crossed by swords?).

They reached what looked like a packaging room—
stamped mints tumbled into the troughs of powdered sugar
before being sent through a massive cylinder that shook
them violently, tumbling the mints out the other side like
jewels; the dead-eyed men scooped them by the handful
into the municipal mint bags that would make their way
into every home.

The Brothers ordered Ben and the other men to sit
against the back wall of the last room, in which they manu-
factured chewing gum. Beneath the peppermint oils used
to infuse the mints, Ben detected stale blood and thawing
meat, smells from the cold rooms of the slaughterhouse
across the courtyard. From where he sat, he could see the
courtyard through a hole in the reinforced glass: butchers
stepped out into the courtyard to smoke, their faces bright
with the cold air of the freezers. They wore black knit caps
and bloodstained coats over doubled-up black sweaters.
They sheathed their massive carving knives in their belts
and lit their cigarettes. Ben could hear workers sweeping up
the powdered sugar along the broad plank floors of the factory with stiff-bristled push brooms; he sat down against the
wall again and looked down the row of men who had been
brought in with him. No one spoke; they didn't pace; they
didn't argue; they just watched the mints tumbling through
machines, bouncing along the factory belts. Some men pretended to sleep. One man was ashamed to be crying and
punched himself repeatedly in the head as if it was simply
malfunctioning, leaking through the eyes. Ben struggled to
swallow in the arid, powdery air of the factory. Somewhere
in the countryside, the innocent trees had been slashed to
bleed sap so that everything in the city could be avalanched
with sugar.

Throughout the day, the Brothers of Mercy marched

men into the room and ordered them against the wall. At dusk, a loud, long horn blasted through the rooms of the factory, and the machines all died at once, as if some great brain had turned black, and the body had fallen slack, and there was silence. More men were brought in, until there was no space left, and Ben was pressed between the wall and the shoulder of an enormous bachelor, and he tried to take sips of fresh air from the little crack in the window.

Ben woke before dawn and listened. The man beside him was snoring; he heard the occasional cough, the hiss of a freezer leaking air in the courtyard, and then the start of a low, intense conversation that spread to dozens of voices, until the room was buried in the din of conversation, halted instantly by the loud cry from outside the doors: "Thanks be to God! It's Independence Day!"

The Brothers of Mercy marched them out of the factory, through the courtyard, and past the hard-set, cold-faced butchers blowing trails of smoke. They marched them through the city streets, so that children could take their rotten aim and men and women, full of mirth on Independence Day, could jeer or frown disapprovingly, depending on disposition. Ben could hear the clamor of the construction site, even before they reached the park. The scrape of shovels, the shouts of men, the racket of machinery operated at full power.

The Brothers of Mercy marched them through the park gates and toward the Independence Day stage. Men in gray smocks were everywhere; Ben had never seen the park so overrun with activity and bodies and confusion. A Brother yanked Ben out of line and said, "Wait here." Ben could hear the trains, leaving frequently for the Sheds, disappearing underground and popping back up again on the other side of the park; he could see the water rushing out into the harbor, see the sheets of lace formed by currents crossing and disrupting one another in their seaward rush. Then the sounds of the train closer, the long, morose horn, the loud, heavy chains bouncing on the empty flatbeds of city trucks. The Brother grabbed Ben again. "Wake up. Come with me." Ben and two other men were taken to the back of the great stage and told to wait. They waited. Ben could smell the burned sugar caught in the engines of the portable icing mixers, the shovels hitting asphalt as workers struck road beneath the mountains of sugar. Workers with sacks of tint walked the line of the icing mixers, inspecting the color, making adjustments, feeding the colored powder into the mixers. A fumigation truck circled the park. The wind picked up and blew apart the clouds of thick smoke that hung in the air. The truck turned and entered the park, rumbling through the muddy, grassy ground, carving out wheel-sized channels. The man standing on the flat bed of the poison truck aimed his poison sprayer at the work crews as he passed. Ben and the other two men took shelter beneath some scrap plywood slanted against the latticework and watched the clouds of chemical smoke spread out. The men in charge dragged them back out—Ben couldn't be sure they were the same men: they had tied handkerchiefs across their faces.

One of the Brothers said, "Line up!" Ben and the other two men lined up. The Brother assessed them, shook his head in disgust. "Listen: you're building steps, the steps up to the stage. The frame's in place—hammer down the planks that form the steps. Do you understand?" The man pointed at Ben—"You hand planks to him" (he pointed to the man at Ben's left); "and you," he said nodding at the man on Ben's right, "stand under the stairs to catch any fallen nails." The odd little man seemed to be entertaining himself with private conversation—"What do you do, Oh, I'm a nail-catcher, I catch nails, Do you ever miss, Well, no one's perfect, but then I collect the nails, I become something of a nail-collector, which is a kind of demotion, but every step of the process is critical . . ." He certainly hadn't stood a chance; at least Ben had been a contender.

The men got into position; the hammerer tested the weight of the hammer in his hand. The little man stood blandly under the framework of the stairs and stared up into the heavens. The heavens watcher turned to the man in charge. He said, "I'm still a man who works with men, my brothers."

"No. You're garbage, and I'm a garbageman," said the Brother in charge. "I'm leaving you to do this work. If you slack off or make a mistake, no matter how minor, I will personally see to it that you are hanged for the crowds this very day. Do you understand?"

Once the Brother was out of earshot, the hammerer turned to Ben. "Ha! Garbageman. 'Yes, 'tis true that I had but one chance to save myself with words,' said he, 'yet I did not choose wisely. Thus begins our sad tale . . .'"

"Please be quiet," said Ben.

Meeks

I sat at the feet of Captain Meeks. Someone had flung a garland of yellow and lavender flowers across the great man's broad metal shoulders; someone had laid bouquets of the same flowers at his feet. The hammering continued as ever.

A few curious onlookers stood in the street and strained to see the state of the park, swarmed over by crews of workers and policemen and a few enterprising merchants who had fibbed their way past the policemen at the gate. I thought of the sacrifices Captain Meeks had made, all those years ago, for these people, myself included, and I hoped that beneath the seasonal excitement crackled a gratitude and a deep acceptance of the terms of his sacrifice. The great man had detected something beautiful, even in the darkness of those days, and the great man had seen that there was something worth salvaging in the city, worth saving in his people. I was mindful of the ominous responsibility that had been placed on my shoulders by Bedge, to represent, as a mere human being with limited time and other resources even more strictly curtailed, so massive and complex and world-altering a set of circumstances as those that surrounded the Captain. I considered, too, that I would be playing my namesake, stepping, as it were, into my own shoes at last.

I pressed my hand flat against the cool grass and closed my eyes and managed to summon the eerie certainty that my mother's palm was pressing against mine from inside the ground. I stood. I was due at the station for the final fitting of my jacket and for other preliminary matters. As I walked toward the station, dragging my feet (my body felt heavy and my legs weak), I passed city artisans detailing the cake. One pair of workers was encrusting the dark boughs of the icing trees with yellow sugar flowers, while another layered the blue-gray frost of harbor waves advancing.

Ben

Ben and the hammerer removed their smocks, and the heavens watcher gasped. "My, God. You're bleeding . . ." Ben looked down at his undershirt—a map of blood. He touched it tentatively. "It's OK. This is old; it's dry."

Ben handed the hammerer a plank, and the hammerer held it close to his face and inhaled deeply. "I love the smell of just-sawed wood." He placed a few nails carefully between his teeth and hammered the first plank onto the framework of the stairs. "Plank," he said, and replaced the nails in his mouth. The heavens watcher stood under the open stairs and shifted his gaze from the open sky to Ben. "I'm awfully hungry," he said. "Aren't you hungry?" Ben and the hammerer ignored him.

Then Ben said, "I wish I had something good, like an orange or a plum."

"Why not wish for an entire tree?" said the hammerer. "Besides I prefer apples."

"Everyone prefers apples," said Ben.

"The other man did what?" shouted the heavens watcher.

"What?"

"Not you."

"Another."

"Bananas, plums, oranges," said Ben. "Something more interesting."

"Another plank," said the hammerer through clenched teeth.

Ben handed over another plank. "We had an apple tree in our yard when I was a boy."

"Plank."

"Actually—want to hear a funny story?" said Ben.

"You wouldn't listen to me," mumbled the hammerer through a mouthful of nails. He hammered down another plank. "You told me to be quiet."

"But it's a story about apples; you'll like it."

"Fine, tell a story. Everyone likes a story. But I'm not following you down some private memory lane, letting you bring us down."

The heavens watcher interrupted. "There once was a man marooned on an island. Everything on the island was black: the sand, the rocks, the cliffs that plunged down into the black water."

"Interesting . . ." said the hammerer. "Go on."

Ben thought of Finton's drawing. "Where is this story from?"

"It's from his *brain*. What do you care?" snapped the hammerer. "Now be quiet, so help me God, and listen—the story has started. Give me another plank, and you," he said, pointing the handle of the hammer at the heavens watcher, "go on."

"The man watched the black waves creep along the black shore and tried to think. He couldn't remember anything about himself—his name or where he had come from or what had happened to him. He seemed to be alone except for three gaunt horses standing in the mouth of a shallow cave. Salt had encrusted their manes and their backs, and the gray horse looked as if it had been cast in metal. The two chestnut horses carved from dark, oil-smoothed wood. A heavy, freezing rain rolled over the island; the black waves bloated with green air crashed and sizzled against the rocks. The swells rolled ahead: all the great moments of history were passing him by. He had fallen out of the world some-how—"

"Through sin!" said the hammerer. "Plank."

"That's right, Brother. *The world has forgotten about me*, the man thought bitterly. The horses stood in a row, rain dripping from their bony heads and their tangled manes; they watched him, and the man came to think of them as his disciples, and sometimes he thought of them as the judges of his life. *I've done nothing wrong!* he shouted at them whenever a black rain rolled over the little island and drenched the black soil, the black rocks, the black—"

"The black clouds, the black pebbles, the black leaves," said Ben impatiently. "We get it."

The hammerer and heavens watcher studied Ben. "You'll note, I said nothing about trees on the island," said the heavens watcher and continued. "The man's mind started filling up with the pictures of another life, another place—sometimes they seemed like memories and sometimes like prophecies, but he hid from the horses that he was often confused. He felt that he was descended from a great people, and he spoke often about the greatness of his people, but the horses only watched him sleepily through heavily lidded eyes. Their heads hung low, giving them an air of skepticism. They were beasts. The man imagined the horses swarming the fields and wrecking the doors of the ancestral home he suddenly remembered. If the chestnut horses had their way, the waves would be lathed from soft, smooth wood; the metal horse would have the clouds careening like ships and collapsing like bridges.

"In the stir of emotion, the man remembered his mother—in fact, he remembered that she was the last thing he had seen before waking up on the island. She had been comforting him, and in that comfort, he had lost the will to survive. His mother's fingernails had combed against his scalp. He had wanted her to find the seams of his head, to pull the loose threads, to break down his head and then his body into smaller and smaller pieces in her lap. He had wanted to be disassembled softly on his mother's lap, and he had wanted it more than he had ever wanted anything in life . . . he was half-asleep, still aware of the trampled-grass smell of her clothes, the feel of sunny wool against his cheek. He wanted to feel his mother breathing and to hear his mother's voice, though not necessarily to understand the words.

"The man jumped to his feet and picked up a water-sharpened black rock. He walked to the mouth of the cave, and he raised the rock over the head of one of the horses. The other two horses stepped away and stood together. The man hammered the rock down onto the head of the horse."

"Bam!" shouted the hammerer and pounded the wooden frame with all his strength. Ben jumped, badly startled, and dropped a plank at the heavens watcher's feet. "Keep quiet," said Ben. "You'll get us in trouble. And hand me the plank."

"I'm only supposed to pick up nails."

"Pick it up!"

"You pick it up. I'm telling a story. . . ."

"Yes, be quiet. He's telling a story."

Ben crawled back down the stairs to retrieve the plank as the heavens watcher continued, "The horse's skull was surprisingly hard and thick, and the man had to hit him again and again. It was horrible. The horse sank to the ground, hesitatingly at first, and then resolutely. The other horses stared uncomfortably at the black soil. If they had thoughts of revenge, they kept those thoughts to themselves. An agonizing hunger forced the man to cut open the belly of the dead horse and eat."

"What part of the horse did he eat first, Father?" the hammerer asked in a small voice.

"Why, he ate the heart, Son!" boomed the heavens watcher.

"What are you even *talking* about?" hissed Ben. "Be quiet. Keep hammering."

"One day, a ship passed near the island, and the man dove into the water and swam toward it. Sailors pulled him aboard, and the man sank to the dry, warm deck. The sailors brought him some hard bread and a cup of hot tea, and he told them about his time on the black island. Three horses— one gray, two chestnut—had control of the island at first; they were so many, and he was so few. *I became very afraid,* he said firmly, *and very hungry.* He had picked up a sharp rock. He had hunted down one horse and then another. Seeing that the bodies of his two friends had been consumed by the man, the gray horse jumped into the water and swam. *Unexpected,* said the man. *Seeing the horse swimming alone, swimming, swimming nowhere. I knew he'd never make it.* The man hid his eyes from the sailors, ashamed that they had filled with tears.

"The man pulled himself together and said, *Let's go home!* His cup of tea trembled in his hands. *My home, my home . . .* The man stared into the wheat-colored tea and tried to concentrate. *God, what's the name?* He tapped his forehead with one of his sharp, bony fingers. Finally he shook his head in embarrassment. *I'll have to describe it to you. Everything is black—the sand, the rocks; the black waves creep along the shore. It's beautiful.* The sailors looked away, embarrassed; they consulted with each other quietly, smiling reassuringly at the man as they whispered to each other. Finally, a young sailor approached and laid a comforting hand on the man's shoulder and said, *Yes, we have seen this place—it feels good to remember.*"

The hammerer was standing on a completed step,

the hammer slack in his hand. "It really does feel good to remember," he said dreamily.

"But you're remembering *nothing*," said Ben. "It doesn't even exist."

"Sure, it does, and you know it. Though, you hate apples, which already makes you some kind of monster. You hate islands, horses, sailors . . . everything, maybe." The hammerer filled his mouth with fresh nails and knelt back down. "Plank!"

Ben handed him another plank of wood. What did it mean, what was he supposed to do? Should he go back to the house and look for Finton? Was Ben the sailor in the story? Was he one of the horses? The hammerer hammered down the plank and addressed the heavens watcher. "Yes, indeed. That's a very complicated situation, philosophically, for the man," he said brightly. "Ever done any acting?" The hammerer filled his mouth with fresh nails.

"No," answered the heavens watcher and shrugged modestly. The hammerer turned to Ben. "You?"

"Never," he answered indignantly.

The hammerer spit his mouthful of nails to the ground (the heavens watcher dropped to his knees and began collecting them). "Well, I am a professional actor, and before you consign us both to the notion that my forced participation on this work crew represents some kind of a professional failure, please know that I revel in the opportunity, however unintentionally garnered, to build with my own hands the boards, the stage, the platform, the great, broad deck upon which the finest, truest words will be spoken. Will I speak them today? Will I speak them tomorrow? Will I ever speak them? I can't know the answer. Yet I know they can't be spoken or heard without this contraption. This!" The hammerer pounded the plank twice with his fist.

"Everything we say should matter," he said, "yet it *doesn't.*"

"Fine. I'm sorry," said Ben.

"What's that?"

"I said, I'm sorry."

"Pardon?"

"Sorry!"

"See what I mean? Hand me another plank. We're almost done here."

Ben handed over another plank of wood and caught a splinter at the base of his thumb. He winced and examined his hand, pinching out the blond sliver with his fingernails.

"God, you're an amateur," said the hammerer. "Just the kind of man people love to make an example of. You should keep your thoughts to yourself, unless you want to climb these steps again tonight. Plank."

Ben was thinking.

"Plank!"

Ben looked up. The hammerer stood, staring, breathing heavily, the hammer hanging heavily in his hand. "Are you not hearing me?"

"What?"

"Another!"

When they had finished the steps, Ben and the other two men were marched to the sidelines, where hundreds of other new civil servants waited in the shade of the old park trees. Ben sat with the hammerer on a massive ridged root. He watched the birds circling over the stage in the mild autumn light; he listened to the park filling up with the shouts of policemen, the excited chatter of the hundreds, the exclamations of children. The distant sounds of a train picking up speed over the rumble-planks in the warehouse district echoed indifferently down the street.

The park was soon packed, families and new couples and young bachelors arranging themselves expertly in the vast clearing before the stage. They gazed at the stage, waited for the Lovers Play to begin. The long gray line of civil servants gazed into the audience, seeking out familiar faces. Ben stood on the root and looked for her, inflicting on himself, in the process, the faces of the smitten and peaceful young, every last one of them a victim of that pleasant bewilderment in others, which is love. Ben saw Selfridge in the crowd, serenely sweatered and stretched out on a boldly checkered red-and-blue picnic cloth, a young woman leaning over him, studying his appetites. Handsome couples were everywhere, a sea of cheerful sweaters and fine fabrics and the soft wool geometries of blankets brought from home. *My life!* She was out there somewhere, if only he could see her, in from her country estate, perhaps curled sweetly beside some brute, some sport, some pal, some normal and happy guy, the man whom she was saving because he was so obviously worth saving. Why, after all, thought Ben, save me? Why save or preserve upon the surface of the earth such a perverse and pointless creature?

"Want to hear something funny?" asked the hammerer, still seated upon the root and experimenting with cuffing the coarse, roomy sleeves of his work smock. How had Ben's life, which his mother had guarded like the last known quantity of the earth's most precious ore, been so easily fused with this *nothing*, a man who acted as if he had lost nothing, because he had nothing, and now, thought Ben, he has the satisfaction of high company in the void.

"Not in the least," said Ben, glaring down at him.

"Fine, then I'll find someone who *will* listen," said the hammerer, jumping up as if on official business and disappearing down the line.

Meeks

Meeks! said Bedge when I arrived. I was happy to see him. Columns of paper covered the desks of several officers; policemen rolled speedily from cabinet to desk, desk to cabinet. End-of-season madness, said Bedge jovially. I followed him down the hall into the small room at the back of the station. The enormous wooden table was bare, the empty chairs lined up neatly against the wall. Bedge left me alone in the room for a few minutes and returned with a black jacket. The black fabric shone, as if cut and polished from a secret mine of perfect stone.

We both turned to look at the window when we heard a swell of sound and the kind of conversation associated with large, poorly organized crowds.

They must have opened the gates, said Bedge. He looked at me—I had clasped my hands together, as if in prayer, to keep them from trembling visibly. Bedge asked if I was nervous. I admitted that I was—I reminded him that I was not accustomed to speaking in front of large crowds but rather tended to watch them from a considerable distance.

Bedge put his hand on my shoulder reassuringly, and he said, Everything will be all right. Listen to me—you'll change into your costume, and you'll wait here. You'll stay here through the opening and the Lovers Play and through lunch—

I need to be outside! I shouted. I had never missed an Independence Day in my life. I had never raised my voice at Bedge. We regarded one another in stunned silence, enjoying the sense of wonder still possible between old friends. My heartbeat spiked with affection—after all these years, we could still surprise one another.

You will be outside, he said, you will be—toward the

end. But we can't very well have the characters walking around in costume, walking around like ordinary people, confusing matters—that wouldn't work. Your job is to make people feel free to feel that whatever is happening to *them* is real. Do you see what I mean? (Of course I did.) I'll come back to collect you for the Founders Play.

I nodded.

As Bedge opened the door of the room to go, something crossed my mind—But where are the other actors? Bedge turned and gestured loosely toward the ceiling.

They're around, he said and left. I heard the lock click, and then I heard Bedge walking down the long hall.

I removed my own jacket and laid it on the table; I put on the tailor-made black jacket, surprisingly light and thin and coarse. I strained to open the window farther, without luck. I knelt on the ground so that I could look through the sliver of open window. I saw the legs and shoes of people as they hurried into the park. When my knees began to ache, I sat against the wall, just beneath the window, and stared sadly at my hands.

Of course it was the sadness of a dream achieved, and in addition to that sadness, which is an unfortunate byproduct of the machinery in place to make the long-dreamed things suddenly true, there is the profound loneliness of a leader of people. Gone were the days of easy affection for other people, gone were the complex camaraderies of the police department. This glumness was a human luxury, a luxury in a moment to be disavowed forever, for what I had discovered was most true in my assumption of the role of the great man was surprising: I had never felt farther away from my people.

I moved one of the chairs close to the window so that I could sit comfortably by resting my elbows on my knees and still see. I trained my eyes upon the slot of fresh air below the heavy window, low and immovable in its sash. The shadows of the trees shifted along the glass, vague, changing, in collusion with certain of my senses to generate a picture of fear. The collar of the coat was rough against my neck; I disliked the strong chemical smell that emanated from the fabric. I imagined I could hear the Lovers Play; rather I deduced from the sudden silence of the crowd that they had become absorbed in something greater than themselves. I sighed discontentedly in the stuffy room. This arrangement was at odds with my happily sentinel nature.

I heard a voice: What'd they get you for?

I craned my neck wildly, searched the room.

What's the charge? (I saw him then: the gray shape of a man standing on the other side of the thick glass of the window. I knelt so that I could see him better—I could make out his left elbow, his hands rising into view to roll a cigarette.)

I'm not a prisoner, I whispered.

You seem *imprisoned*, he said.

No, no. I'm not under arrest. I'm just waiting in the wings, so to speak. I've got a part in the play.

Lovers?

No, Founders.

Huh.

What's happening now?

Am I allowed to tell you?

Of course you're allowed to tell me. The real question is, Am I allowed to tell you?

Tell me what?

That I'm Captain Meeks, for crying out loud. I'm playing the Captain.

All right, all right. Let's see . . . the audience is watching the Lovers Play, soaking up the same old sentimental shit. What a waste. Are you a professional actor?

No.

Classic. Because I *am* a professional actor, currently unemployed.

You didn't get a part?

No, sir. That would suggest there was some justice in this rotten world.

I searched my mind for a helpful reply (I knew how lucky I was). Perhaps they think it will be more realistic this way, I ventured.

Realistic? The actor stormed off, but only a very short distance. I suppose that's in their training. I could smell the smoke from his cigarette; I let him be. The closer the hour drew, the more I worried that I was out of my league. I wished Bedge would appear so that we could discuss alternatives. Perhaps this unhappy and unemployed actor would like a shot at playing the Captain? The work of an actor was a great responsibility, no matter how frivolously actors, in general, conducted their private lives. The failure of even the minorest characters to play their roles with sufficient conviction might cause the entire production to disintegrate.

Psst, I said. And then, *Excuse me please.*

What? answered the voice flatly after a delay.

Do you have any advice?

He hesitated. I try to be innocent of everything except the words I'm speaking.

I should protest my innocence?

Not unless the character has been written to protest his innocence. Though that doesn't necessarily mean he's innocent. It gets very complicated. But any *trained actor* can easily tell the difference. (I heard the man rasp his calloused hands together in the faint chill of the air, and then silence.)

Hello? I called out to no one.

After a decent interval, there was thundering applause and cheers, and the sound of inveterate conversationalists tuning their instruments. I peered again through the open window and could see a portly father unfurling a soft blanket on the ground as his children looked on skeptically. Families new and old were arranging their objects and appetites around the afternoon picnic. There was the hum of many voices operating agreeably and cooperatively toward pleasure, and though I was tense with anticipation—possibly stage fright, I admitted to myself—I fell into a deep and sudden sleep that pulled me from the chair. I was startled by my collision with the ground, concluded that I was on the floor unexpectedly, and, in the next instant, I lost consciousness.

Bedge came to collect me, as he had promised. My neck ached from having slept so soundly and awkwardly on the hard floor of the police station. Bedge dusted off my dark coat fussily.

What happened here? he kept asking and clicking his tongue with disapproval.

I'm sorry, I said. I shook my head. I was trying to wake up, to clear my mind. While I was in this state of mild confusion, which was, frankly, a blessing, in that it had deadened my nerves, Bedge led me out of the station.

Ben

"Where *were* you?" Ben took the hammerer by the collar of his smock.

"Hands *off*." Ben released him, imprisoned his angry hands in his pockets. "I just went for a walk. What's the big deal?"

"The big deal," said Ben, "is that the three of us are responsible for each other, and if they'd come to check on us and said, 'Where's your brother?' then it would have been over for us, and you'd be off walking around in a dream. Actors!"

"You really need to relax. You understand they've already *got* us, right? That it couldn't get any worse?"

The heavens watcher was lying in the grass, listening; he looked up at the hammerer. "I tend to agree with you, but, really, it could get worse. God knows what happens in the prison, and there's that," he said, pointing to the coiled rope high among the branches.

Ben turned his back on them and sat back on the root. He watched the newly minted mothers and fathers, the newly minted husbands and wives, folding their blankets neatly and scooping up their picnic baskets and leaving the ground littered in pistachio shells and discarded fat from their sandwiches and orange peels and apple cores.

"We'll have to clean all this, I suppose," said the hammerer.

"Or eat it," said the heavens watcher and tried to reach out discreetly for a leathery nub of salami.

The hammerer sat beside the heavens watcher. "Want to hear some gossip?"

"I suppose."

"Guess who's playing Captain Meeks this year?"

"You?"

"Well, funnily enough, I *was* going to be in the play this year. My dear brother was supposedly arranging everything. Where would be if not for our dear brothers, Brothers?"

"Then who's playing the Captain?"

"The park bum!"

The heavens watcher shrugged. "Good for him."

"And bad for me—but no point in being bitter. I was genuinely hopeful, and it seemed things were about to change for me. Things didn't change. Except to get worse. But I'm still optimistic that things might *yet* change for me. You see? The artist's heart is eternally open to disappointment."

"And brothers still steal from brothers, still delight in fooling and exploiting one another," added the heavens watcher.

"A brother must serve his brother, but he must also serve himself, live as if he has no brothers," said Ben over his shoulder.

"Where's that from?" asked the heavens watcher.

"My brain," said Ben.

"I take it you have no brothers?" said the hammerer. "Which would explain your refreshingly philosophical take on brotherhood." He slammed the hammer down on the hard root of the tree and searched the crowd. "Where is my dear brother, anyway?"

"Relax," said Ben. "They could yank any of us from the crowd."

"They should take me," said the heavens watcher suddenly and stared at his hands.

The hammerer shook his head. "Easy, Brother. You're a good man. Whatever it is you think you've done, I guarantee you we've done worse."

"Speak for yourself," said Ben. "I did nothing wrong; I

was betrayed."

"What is *wrong* with you, Brother? Not *everyone* is out to get you—only them," he said, and pointed to the Brothers of Mercy, who were starting to make their way through the crowd: "Brothers and Sisters! Come together, come together!"

The heavens watcher covered his face. "I stole another man's suit from his closet while he was sleeping. I might as well have killed him with my bare hands. He's here some- where, I'm sure, smocked just like me."

Ben looked away immediately. The hammerer put his arm around the heavens watcher. "It's OK, Brother. We've all ended up in the same place. Don't be so hard on yourself."

"We'd better go. It's starting," said the heavens watcher and got to his feet. Ben and the hammerer stood, and they walked with everyone else toward the stage. The men in the trees worked their theatrical ropes, generating peals of metallic thunder and the hollow chop of heavy boats moving through the shallows of the harbor toward shore. There was the pounding, hoisting step of powerful axles building speed, the hard scrape of machinery dragging itself out of the water and through a bramble of branches. Almond-shaped shadows drifted across the stage and into the streets; searchlights swept over the crowd, just as the lanterns had pierced the fog on that famous moonless night.

Two policemen led a group of men in dark suits toward the stage steps. Ben felt the crowd surge forward. He and the other men surged forward with the crowd.

"Oh, my God. It is him," said the heavens watcher, sounding suddenly frail.

"Who?"

"The man I killed."

Ben saw Finton among the prisoners, too. He was stooped, dazed, in a humiliating black suit. Ben wished he had never seen it. He looked away, pretended to study the Old Row of Bachelor Houses. The wind picked up and passed over the ivy-covered facades of the buildings until the row of old houses looked like the surface of the dark green river, disrupted by gusts. The wind pushed its way through the rows of trees in the park; the leaves on the trees shook noisily and then went soft.

The heavens watcher covered his face, "I can't watch this happen. I'll die! I'm going to volunteer. Or else I want you to take that hammer and crush my skull."

"Get a hold of yourself," said the hammerer.

"You don't understand. I was such a profound disappointment to my mother, who was a *saint*. I've broken every heart I ever touched."

"But have you really touched that many?"

"Many."

"Where are you going?" Ben heard the hammerer's terrified whisper behind him, as he started walking toward the corral of prisoners. "Stop, Ben. Stop now."

Meeks

A great roar rose from the crowd when Bedge and I came into view. I lowered my head, suddenly overcome by self-consciousness. The people came to life, jostling one another energetically behind the human barricade of broad-bodied policemen. I glanced up uncertainly, and Bedge smiled conspiratorially at the reception we were being given.

I could see the factories, like a majestic fleet of beautiful white ships forever cresting our horizon, the tireless engines of industry, the cloudlets of steam rising from the stacks. I heard the wind through the trees, smelled the sugar in the air, saw young women sipping their sunny lemon drinks, and I was happy again, happy to be outside beneath the trees, happy to see the people, all the amusing variations on existence arrayed before me. Bedge led me to the platform and signaled that I should wait at the base of the stairs. He bounded up the steps to take his place onstage. Bedge peered into the crowd until every conversation had died under his silent gaze, and the people were silent and still.

Listen, Brothers and Sisters!

We are listening!

Captain Meeks saved us from the Enemy. Do you know this story?

Yes, but we want to remember!

Let us always tell this story to one another!

Yes, it feels good to remember!

The words Bedge spoke passed over my brain in a wave that was almost nauseating in its familiarity. He reminded us that Captain Meeks alone had the wisdom and strength to perceive a true Enemy across the water, to call him out into the light. So long as we kept the Captain's ways, we would be safe.

The Enemy is always watching us! Bedge bellowed. From across the water, from the edge of the woods, can you see his savage eyes in the dark? He is waiting, Brothers and Sisters, waiting for us to grow lazy, to lie down in defeat. We must never give up!

We will never give up!

Bedge reminded us that unhappiness and turmoil and contradiction can proliferate only in the dissatisfied and unfulfilled heart, and that in the rogue and questioning heart, the Enemy could still find purchase, settle in, start to destroy us, one by one.

Ours is a world formed by love, by the loving word of Captain Meeks!

Let us be grateful to the Captain!

Bedge paused, allowing an expected solemnity to spread through the crowd. But there's a problem, sighed Bedge. Some hearts refuse to be whole, cannot be made whole again. Some people have been unhappy.

We confess that sometimes we have been unhappy!

I have told you about how the Enemy lives across the water?

You have told us!

I have told you about how doubt endangers our hearts?

You have told us!

I tell you now that we must destroy that doubt within ourselves, and we must learn what that doubt looks like in others, whom it inhabits.

We believe you!

And I'm telling you that the Enemy is living right here among us. Never forget that!

We will never forget!

Do you know why we gather in this way each year?

To remember the First Day!

Yes. And just as Captain Meeks, on the First Day, brought the Enemy to this place and hanged him so that we could be free, so each year, we bring our Enemy to this place and hang him, so that we can *remain* free.

Like all people, I felt most exhilaratingly contaminated by doubt in the final moments before the Enemy of our hopes was symbolically destroyed. Soon our hearts would be pure again, free of all the error and curiosity about other ways of living that had crept in. The Brothers of Mercy let loose a hail of words: Let's work, Brothers! Let us do this work today!

I watched Bedge keenly, hung on his every word. I remembered so well being a boy, when I used to shudder at the ominous words of the old Chief of Police, when I used to bury my face in my mother's lap and beg her to tell me that everything would be all right.

The moment was drawing near when I would climb the steps and stand before the people and speak for the Captain. In keeping with tradition, I would frown like the Captain, square my shoulders like the Captain, boom my voice like the Captain, and say, I want you to be free, Brothers and Sisters. There is no sacrifice too great. Then I would look around for the Condemned Man. Is it you, I would say, No, they would say, Is it you, I would say, No, they would say.

I wondered . . . how does a Condemned Man really think and feel? Does he take stock of the world, even in jest, collect everything he knows, so that he can take it with him when he goes? And would this be a loving or vengeful act in a man condemned to death, the hoarding of reality in the old, cold hold, only to capsize the ship?

Then what happens? I used to ask my mother.

The Condemned Man has been hanged.

Then what happens?

Nothing.

For the first time in my life, I doubted my mother or simply wished that she was wrong.

I was trying to think of what might happen next. I remembered that one year, when I was very young, I wandered off into the crowd, determined to get a closer look. How did they accomplish this elaborate illusion; where was the contraption that made it possible for the hanged man to seem to die (but, in fact, to be saved)? I reached the front of the crowd easily; I was small and determined. A young policeman, a rookie, smiled down at me. I was pinned between the rowdy crowd and him. What's your name? he asked. My name is Meeks! (These seemed to be the first or best words I had ever spoken, even now.) I'm Bedge, he said, and he patted me gently on the head. In the next moment, the bells rang out, and the crowd pulsed forward, knocking me to the ground. I was instantly terrified, separated from my mother. I could hear the hooves of the police horses scraping noisily on the street; I was afraid I would be trampled. Bedge scooped me up and carried me to a safe spot under the stage. I lay on the ground and peered into the shadows under the stage. The Condemned Man was still swaying slowly in the mouth of the trap door, the taut rope creaking. *Hello?* I said, but his face was hidden by the black hood. Then the Brothers of Mercy appeared and started to cut the man down—one of them saw me hiding, and I scrambled out from under the stage and ran again.

I ran out of the park and hid in the doorway of a old building. The streets were empty; a yellow bulb swung overhead, slicking the shadows with oily yellow light that revolted me. I could hear the chaos of the multitudes in the park, but I was being forced by events to test on my heart a new hypothesis—that I might be completely alone in the universe. It was getting cold and dark. The wind was picking up. A figure was headed for me; I raised myself up and peered: Mother? Rather, it was the man in the black jacket. The collar of his shirt fluttered against his neck. I thought optimistically, Perhaps Mother has sent him to rescue me. He glanced at me coldly, as I shivered with terror in the doorway, and he walked on. I knew better than to call out to him.

A man cleared his throat noisily beside me. Bedge had brought over another actor and ordered him to stand beside me; we were standing shoulder to shoulder at the base of the platform steps.

Trade jackets, whispered the other actor.

Pardon me?

Let's trade costumes—you take mine, and I'll take yours.

No way. Never, I said, continuing to look straight ahead, and I shook my head in disbelief. Even a novice to the stage knows better than to break this most basic rule.

But I couldn't resist knowing what my options were. I turned to study his costume—a Condemned Man? The Bell Ringer? He was a frail man, aged beyond his years, wearing a beautifully tailored dark suit. He turned to face me. I stared into his eyes. His hand shook slightly as he pointed at my chest.

You, he said, should trust *me*, and he turned his pointing hand upon himself.

I stared at the man standing beside me. I was face-to-face with the man in the black jacket. Bedge had granted me my only wish in life, and I heard myself say, I should trust *you*? (Why in life's biggest moments, when what I say should matter most, do I resort helplessly to repetition?)

It's not too late, he said earnestly. He tried to hand me his props—the theatrical hood, a length of rope. Quickly, he said. He reached out to touch my elbow, and I flinched.

Meeks.

Yes, that's right, I answered blandly, I will be playing the Captain. (I felt very far away from myself.)

No—you: Meeks.

Again you amaze me with your powers of observation. You are correct: I am playing Captain Meeks.

Trade with me, he pleaded. Let me go in your place.

I shook my head no—of course, now that I finally had something worthwhile, something of inestimable value, he had returned to take it from me. You must think I'm a great fool, I said.

I promised your mother I'd take care of you.

What a joke, I said, and rolled my eyes for good measure, but I was suddenly close to tears.

Please, Meeks. Take these things from me.

Bedge came clomping back down the platform steps and stopped directly before me. The crowd was silent. He laid his hands on my shoulders and met my eyes; I knew that once we ascended the stairs he would be lost to me forever.

Bedge, I said.

Meeks, he answered.

I turned to look at the man in the black jacket. He gave Bedge a final, long, desperate look and whispered, Let me go in his place! Bedge and I ignored him, and I turned to follow Bedge up the stairs to the stage, though my thoughts, to be truthful, were suddenly in a frightening state of disarray, scrambling for safe and solid places to alight. Think of your mother, I instructed myself as I climbed the stairs. Then I thought of my mother, only of my mother, imagined the cool, light pressure of her hand against my forehead.

Ben

Ben stared at the ground and pushed his way through the crowd. Young men shoved him; young women recoiled at the sight of his haggard face, his hanging gray smock, his bloodstained undershirt. He could feel the men in the trees watching him.

As he approached the corral of prisoners, a policeman stepped in his way, laid a hand forcefully on his shoulder. "You're in the wrong place, Brother. Go back to the worker area unless you'd rather be a prisoner." Ben was too terrified to look. The policeman turned him around by the shoulders and kicked him in the seat of his pants. "That way!"

Ben walked; the people parted slightly as he went, and he followed the channel opening up before him. He was *willing* to sacrifice himself, but his will was forever the hostage and lackey of the brutal, soulless survivor who ran things in his head. A cloud dragged its shadow like a net across the trees, across the light gray backs of the birds that had settled along the branches. Ben could see the Brothers of Mercy walking along the periphery of the crowd, searching for someone. Perhaps the others had said something; he wanted immediately to run. Hold your ground, his brain instructed sternly, and he managed to hold his ground by closing his eyes and pretending he was elsewhere. All of humanity was absorbed in the events of the day, save him, who had discovered in himself the freedom to occupy other scenarios, other moments, at will. Every other creature of this world—the men, the women, the horses, the birds, the beetles, the bees, the moths, the squirrels—were just the things he had invented for himself. The dark gray buildings, the yellow-glowing windows, the rows of trucks, the watchful policemen, the untrustworthy brothers, the gusting postcards, the swaying ropes, the fruit-laden branches rising in succession like an archway of swords, like a series of curtains parting: they were all his.

"Move aside! Step back!" Ben could hear the Brothers of Mercy making their way through the crowd; he opened his eyes and watched them pass at a safe distance. He was as good as dead, but he still had possession of his body, a fungible corpse he could choose to trade in for something better in this world. If he ran toward the stage, he could reach it in time, be hanged in an innocent man's stead. His body refused to move.

The sun was setting, casting everything in a blue-gray light, the evening air subsuming more and more, until this world would be reduced to a meaningless thicket of shadows: rock indistinguishable from man, earth from sea. The world was disappearing, thing by thing, the evening steadily repossessing all the objects that the daylight had made to seem permanently stowed among Ben's own effects. The lavender spaces between the dark green leaves were flooding with ink, the shapes of leaves fusing together in the failing light. Men would be consolidated with their hats, with the tools of their trades; women would be consolidated into blocks of shadow with the men, their children circling them frantically in the failing light. Ben checked his shirt. The buttons were still bright, the cuffs luminescent; he had not yet been subsumed. Ben's mother had once given him a blank book, a book in which to write his thoughts. He had never written in it. He looked overhead at the clouds, flat and bright against the evening sky. He remembered: he had upset his mother; to spite her he had torn the blank pages of his book and thrown them into the river.

"Step aside! Let us through!" The Brothers of Mercy coming closer. If he ran hard across the park and kept to the river, he might be able to reach the wilderness beyond the prison and take refuge among the unnavigable pines.

"There! Stop right there!" Ben waited to feel their claws on his back, to be wrestled brutally to the ground. Then he saw her—as if the Brothers of Mercy had guided his eyes to the very spot. She was walking alone through the crowd, as if hiding from someone or seeking them out. She walked faster; Ben watched her. He felt happy, then hurt, then angry, then worried—was she in trouble? Don't be ridiculous, he chided himself, she has everything in this world, and you have nothing. Did she help you when you needed it most? He was not marooned in this world. He would not be simply forgotten! Let her see him. Let her *see* him. Let everyone see him, let them finally get it: when something is lost, it's lost forever.

Meeks

I stood in silence beside Bedge on the high platform. Pairs of workers walked along the cake, carrying the fiery lengths of rope between them, igniting the candles as they went, and then throwing the rope into the river where it slapped the surface and steamed. I gazed down the steps at the man in the black jacket. What on earth was my mother thinking when she entrusted my safety to this frail and fearful creature? I wished I had never pursued the matter, that I had let it rest, that I had concentrated on a future made of something other than the ancient past.

I wanted nothing more than to return to my former routines—I was still as curious as I had ever been about the city and the people in it. I wanted to descend the platform steps immediately and be among them again, to walk with the furiousness of a private purpose through the park, as I often had when I was happy. I strained to see distant details in the growing dark. I searched the windows of the buildings on the grand avenue. What *was* that infinitesimal light glowing within them?

Bedge was talking about the history of our great city, as depicted on the cake, glowing like a river of well-meaning light below us. There was Captain Meeks carrying his mother's body through the flood-blue streets. Captain Meeks walking unperturbed beneath the deep blue water; a clutch of icing bubbles overhead that bloomed to puffs of clean steam on the surface and fed the machines on the nearby piers. He walked along the ocean floor, harvesting mussels by hand, tossing them into a net that trailed behind him for dozens of feet. The net was filled with bricks, wheat, pheasants, goats, gold, stone, trees, rain clouds, salmon, reeds, horses, fire, and yellow rosettes of stars he plucked as lazily as peaches from the firmament as he crossed the mountain ranges, when he had the joy of a mountaineer! Captain Meeks in the bleak, bulb-lit rooms by the piers, lecturing from atop the butcher-block tables (he was explaining a new world, understanding it). Captain Meeks by the river pointing to the trees, to the earth. Young women stared seriously wherever he pointed; young men stared seriously wherever he pointed. Captain Meeks lassoing and saddling the wild horses and stooping to feed their foals. Captain Meeks shooting birds out of the blank white sky, climbing trees to cut their nests to the ground with a curved sword. (How could one ever tire of Independence Day or the story of Independence Day?) I stared. As always, I was in awe of the cake, as one cannot help but be awed by the velocity of tradition and by the brutal hugeness of life, in diversified and self-diversifying forms, as it habitates one's hour. Mint-green icing leaves and chocolate-planked trees. Teardrop cookies, pouched in the deep white icing, were the small gray and purple birds that the Captain had blasted out of the brisk, leafless air.

I tilted my head back to see the men high in the Great Tree. I could see their boot soles clearly, as if they were standing on the surface of a clean, cool river and I was looking up from the riverbed. I smiled at the sight, the men hanging about in the trees, rapt, the spectators studying the cake or watching us on the stage. The theatrical workers navigated their ropes, whispering terse directives to one another. I saw the brothers on their branch, the elder brother watching me with cold intensity, the younger muttering apologetically to his hands. My *brothers*.

Bedge cleared his throat; he shifted his weight from one leg to the other. The river emptied forever into the gray harbor. My heart swelled with longing for my mother, with love for the crowd before me. After all these years, the sight of other people could still be the most beautiful.

The Bell Ringer, announced Bedge in a voice that was so successfully theatrical it made my blood run cold. The man in the black jacket regarded me from the bottom of the platform steps, his hands shaking visibly as he clutched the hood, the length of rope. What a heartbreaking disappointment a father could be when one held him up against the beauty and complexity of the world that had existed before him. Perhaps he was no one, only a man who had stolen precious hours from me, time I might have spent with my mother while she was still in this world. The man in the black jacket climbed the wooden steps and was soon beside me. I stared straight ahead, looked deep into the empty streets. I could hear the river emptying into the sea; I could hear the fountain churning, the soothing illusion of infinite action.

In the poor light, the stone facades of the distant buildings looked as if they had been cut from coarse gray paper, and I imagined I could hear the cellophane rustle of counterfeit fires burning in their fireplaces, could reach out and touch anything in the world, no matter how remote. This world, however imperfect, was all that my mother had left me. I was frightened. *Bedge*, I whispered. He ignored me. Rust-colored leaves gusted across the park and toward the river. The air was drafting coolly up from the surface of the water. I could see out of the corner of my eye that the man in the black jacket was trembling, staring at his hands, the tools that they held. My neck ached from the strain of standing at attention before the crowd. The man in the black jacket whispered, *Meeks*. I ignored him.

If I could hold in my mind everyone who had ever hurt my mother and within the final act destroy them, obliterate everyone who had hurt my mother by hurting her only son, perhaps I would. There is no grief as deep as a mother's grief, as never-ending; no one knows her grief but her. Other scenarios, other visions of life, are forever presenting themselves, but one must choose how to live, choose whether or not to betray the people who introduced you first to this world. I knew this story by heart, the story of Captain Meeks and of my brothers and sisters. Was I my own man or was I theirs, or did I belong, eternally, to my mother?

The crowd had begun to chant my name: *Meeks. Meeks. Meeks.*

I was trying to imagine what it would be like to feel the terrible coarseness of the heavy rope as it fell against my neck; I was trying to imagine what it would be like to smell the old fabric of the black hood as it fell across my face, and then I saw a man break away from the shadows and run. What a heartbreaking and beautiful sight! I wanted to call out to him, to shout: Run! Run! A lone figure, his legs pumping wildly as he ran through the dusk toward the black horizon; he ran, turning this way then that, racing toward me, then away, as the Brothers of Mercy gave chase. Look how energetic and hopeful these lifeforms are! How vigorous and blind and greedy to the end, the man churning through the thinning air, the Brothers of Mercy, sleek and holy-looking, closing in on him. Run! Run!

Julia Holmes was born in Dhahran, Saudi Arabia, and grew up in the Middle East, Texas, and New York, where she is an assistant editor at *Rolling Stone*. She is a graduate of Columbia University's MFA program in fiction. *Meeks* is her first novel.